OAXACA, 1998

Other Books by Donley Watt

Can You Get There from Here?

The Journey of Hector Rabinal

Haley, Texas 1959

Reynolds

Dancing with Lyndon

OAXACA, 1998

DONLEY WATT

FORT WORTH, TEXAS

Library of Congress Cataloging-in-Publication Data

Names: Watt, Donley, author.
Title: Oaxaca, 1998 / Donley Watt.
Description: Fort Worth, Texas : TCU Press, [2022] | Summary: "Maggie O'Neill's life in Houston has become a story of loss. Maggie, always in a contentious relationship with her mother, becomes caretaker when the difficult woman is dying of cancer. Maggie's marriage of almost twenty-five years ends in divorce, and her only child has left Houston to find his independence. Maggie is left with little more than her camera, to which she, a novice, warily entrusts her future. Desperate to begin a new life, she drives to Laredo and fights off her doubts as she crosses the border into Mexico. Slowly, the Mexican landscape and people open her eyes to a fresh way of seeing through the lens of her camera. During a stopover in San Miguel de Allende she receives unsolicited advice to go to Casa Azul, Frida Kahlo's house in Coyoacan. In Oaxaca, on impulse, Maggie enrolls in a watercolor class taught by Connor, a visiting Texas artist, and from there the story unfolds through both Maggie's and Connor's eyes. The author's own experiences of living in Oaxaca and his close observation of detail inform the story in a rich, evocative way. - Donley Watt is the author of five books of fiction. His collection of short stories, Can You Get There from Here, won the Texas Institute of Letters prize for best first book of fiction. He has traveled extensively in Mexico and lived for six months in Oaxaca"— Provided by publisher.
Identifiers: LCCN 2021055173 (print) | LCCN 2021055174 (ebook) | ISBN 9780875658025 (paperback) | ISBN 9780875658087 (ebook)
Subjects: LCSH: Man-woman relationships--Fiction. | Oaxaca (Mexico : State)—Fiction. | LCG-FT: Novels.
Classification: LCC PS3573.A8585 O29 2022 (print) | LCC PS3573.A8585 (ebook) | DDC 813/.54--dc23/eng/20211117
LC record available at https://lccn.loc.gov/2021055173
LC ebook record available at https://lccn.loc.gov/2021055174

Cover photo by Lynn Watt

TCU Box 298300
Fort Worth, Texas 76129
To order books: 1.800.826.8911

Design by Preston Thomas

DEDICATION

TO LYNN, FOR HER UNWAVERING SUPPORT

PREFACE

On a Tuesday morning in early November, the city of Oaxaca had just begun to stir. Two men wielding long-handled twig brooms swept their way down Calle Alcalá, the street more littered than most days, since tourists had come to the city to observe (and try to feel as participants) in the Day of the Dead ritual events.

A few blocks north of the *zócalo*, on Alcalá, with its clusters of shops and restaurants, Señora Velez, a stout, energetic woman, the owner of the Galeria de las Tres Palomas, hurriedly searched through storage boxes in the back room of her gallery. Finally, she found what she knew had to be there, a black wreath she had placed on the gallery's front door a few years back, after her husband had collapsed and died while returning uphill from his morning coffee at Del Jardín.

Now she shook the wreath and dust flew; she smoothed out what wrinkles she could. Outside the gallery, a few minutes before that front door would normally open at ten, she hung the black ribbon wreath back on the same hook that had been there since her husband's death. Just below the wreath, her bold, handwritten note in broad, black letters, in Spanish and in English, could be read from the street:

Closed Due to a Death.
Will OPEN again on THURSDAY

Señora Velez stepped back and nodded her approval.

Back inside, she retrieved her purse and flicked off the gallery lights, then locked the front door and left.

CHAPTER 1

From the thirty-third floor of the Allied Bank Building Maggie felt she could see forever. She moved closer to the expanse of windows, fighting off a woozy, dizzying wash of vertigo. It's okay, she told herself, to feel uncomfortable thirty-three floors above Houston's shimmering sidewalks. For windows did pop out of these glass-box buildings now and then; in places as civilized as Boston it happened. There's no telling what might happen here.

And planes fell out of the sky, too, and a woman right here in Houston only yesterday choked to death on a fast food bean and cheese burrito. Life is problematic. Life is precarious. Especially for Maggie O'Neill. Especially right now.

Maggie sighed and stepped even closer to the wall of glass, until her nose touched its clear, smooth coldness, until she felt that with one tiny push she might tumble out into the void. She shuddered, but in a perverse sort of way longed to explode clear of this lawyer's office. Maggie fantasized that she might not plunge to the sidewalk below, but instead right herself and soar in soft circles just beneath the scattering of puffy clouds. From there, high above the streets of Houston, she might clear her head and make intelligible the twists and downward spirals of her life.

Make intelligible? "Uh-uh," Maggie said out loud, for she was alone here, waiting, still waiting in this lawyer's conference room. No, not make intelligible. Make a medium-sized splat, would be more like it. A splat and a tiny mention inside tomorrow's Metro Section. That's what Maggie O'Neill would make.

Out to her right Maggie tried to spot her house—what was still her house—or what would be half her house for a few more minutes, until Robert Livingston III or his secretary bounced back into the room and slid a stack of blue-bound, legal-size papers across the inlaid teak table for her to sign. One more glimpse of her house was all she wanted, the six towering pine trees out front, the bramble of sweet-smelling honeysuckle—always too messy, too out of control for Gordon—that smothered the back fence. The basketball goal at the end of the driveway, its net rotted and tattered away since Kelly had grown up and moved out.

She traced her fingers across the glass, trailing a light smudge. Westheimer ran west out of downtown, and from up there that street below seemed no more than a sliver of pot-holed pavement that fronted a contamination of shops sporting patched tar roofs and florid fronts. Maggie slid her finger on across the window, where Westheimer snaked under the Loop.

But there the smaller side streets disappeared into the cover of trees that smothered her old neighborhood. Oh, well. And all at once Maggie had no interest in the house, anyway. Not any more.

She eased to her left, backing off just a little, trailing her fingers lightly on the glass for balance. Farther to the south the cross-hatched land and smoke and smog of the city dispersed into a gray-blue mass that transfused in some unseen place above the Gulf of Mexico. She wished she could see all the way across that immense body of water to Mexico, for she would be there tomorrow, at the border, anyway. Yes. A tingle of lightness flitted through her. Mexico tomorrow.

But today, within the next hour, some bored and indifferent divorce judge would legally split what she and Gordon had started almost twenty-five years before. Split it asunder. Asunder. That strange word came out of nowhere, from the archaism of her wedding day. "What God hath joined together, let no man put asunder." How quaint, Maggie thought. Well, God or no God, asunder it would be. And Maggie O'Neill will become a single woman for the first time in—well, almost forever, it seemed.

Maggie took a step back and caught her reflection in the tinted glass, but she turned quickly away. For Maggie no longer trusted mirrors, unsure of herself, and of who she was, or might become. Maggie O'Neill, a woman of middle-age, pleasant looking—almost attractive some might say—was dressed more or less appropriately for divorce court. She wore a two-piece rose-colored suit that she swore she would trash and burn after today. Maggie had salvaged some low-heeled pumps from a deep-in-the-closet sack with "for Goodwill" scrawled across it, and her best friend Michelle had loaned her a dressy, one-shade-too-red leather bag that clashed with her suit. Michelle had told her what she already knew—that her handmade-in-Guatemala fanny pack wouldn't do. Not before the judge. "Dress like a lady," Michelle said. "But flash his honor a little knee, girlfriend. Maybe a little thigh. That can do wonders."

Maggie laughed softly, checked the still-shut office door, then turned to confront herself in the window once again. A pair of silver earrings dangled from her ears, hoops that were a little too large, too flashy for an appearance in court; silver hoops she had picked up a year ago—right after Gordon had moved out—in the museum gift shop. The earrings were from Mexico, hand-hammered by a craftsman in Taxco, earrings that Robert Livingston III earlier had spotted right away.

Maggie ignored her lawyer's disapproval, the slight shake of his head, the silver hoops being so much a part of the new Maggie that she had to wear them. This very morning when Maggie held the hoops tentatively to her ears, Michelle had told her, "Girl, those earrings dance!"

The door to the conference room swung open, and Robert Livingston III hurried into the room and dropped the stack of papers on the table between them. He wore navy blue slacks and wingtip shoes; his suspenders bright and garish stripes against the white of his dress shirt. He tilted his head down, peering at Maggie over the tops of his half glasses. He smiled a professional smile. "All over now," he said, "but the signing." Maggie figured he would fill the room with divorce-day, feel-good clichés if she let him. "The glass half full or half empty," or "If you're stuck with lemons, make lemonade" sorts of upbeat bumper stickers of the brain that she had no time for. Too many years had been taken up with such simple-minded nonsense.

Maggie glanced out the window once more before taking the pen her lawyer held out for her. "All over?" she said. "Or maybe it's only the beginning."

That sounded braver than Maggie felt, and she wished she had Kelly's old Pony League baseball cap, the one she wore when she felt beaten down, because it said BRAVES across the front, and she wanted to be brave.

Maggie truly worked at being brave (and she was most the time), holding her braveness close, wrapping herself in her braveness to insulate her from the emptiness, to cover her losses. But Gordon, her soon-to-be-ex, was not a recent loss. Now he was absent from her life, but he was not something to have lost, for he hardly had been there, not for years.

And Kelly had detached himself long ago, the way young men inevitably break from their mothers, although Maggie hadn't realized that until a year or so ago, when he turned twenty-three and was gone. His presence had dripped away, a slow leak, hardly noticeable until one day he had wandered out to New Mexico, leaving Maggie with a small and dry emptiness. A mother's loss.

Not Maggie's only loss. She thought of her mother, gone now less than two years, her body crisscrossed with scars from surgeries meant to heal, but that only disfigured.

Robert Livingston III moved impatiently back and forth while she signed her name, the name now Maggie O'Neill. The signature curled across the documents like a stranger's name, the O'Neill jarring, jumping off each page. This was her old name, her dead father's name once again, as if for more than two decades Maggie had lived under an alias in a foreign land.

The secretary came in and with only a glance at Maggie, began to flip through the instruments—the deed and the agreement and the disclosure and the settlement and the waiver and on and on. Maggie signed them all. The secretary asked, "Do you swear that you executed these documents of your own free will?" and Maggie almost laughed at the absurdity of that question. Free will? Nothing is free, especially Maggie's will. But she nodded, yes, and murmured, "I do swear." Michelle would approve of that, the swearing part. And Maggie could hear Michelle add, "You mother-fuckers." Maggie smiled. The secretary hesitated a moment and frowned in puzzlement.

Maggie turned away. On one wall a line of photographs: a younger Robert Livingston III on some rugby team, not being lawyerly at all; and another, this time older, the lawyer in camouflage, with a gun cradled easily in the crook of one arm. He stood over the propped-up head of a many-pointed, glassy-eyed buck stretched out beneath him on the gray ground; then again, lawyer Livingston holding up a string of glistening red snapper.

On a side table in the room, a couple of obligatory, gold-framed photos. One of the wife, with flipped and frosted hair, a slender nose and slightly bulging eyes—distinctive, striking in a not-quite-handsome sort of way.

4

Maggie's features seemed vague, poorly defined by comparison. She wished for a Roman nose, or, dimples or even a wash of freckles. Anything to keep her from being plain Maggie O'Neill. But she had lively blue-green eyes and full lips and not a bad body at all. Be careful what you wish for, she reminded herself.

The wife in the photo had two boys by her side, the boys in blue blazers, both with lawyer Livingston's confident smiles; a slight gap between the teeth of the older one. Maggie went back to the wife, studied her smile, tried to see if a crack showed anywhere. But the woman, the lawyer's wife, held her smile, by God. So sure of herself. Maggie shook her head in wonder and regret.

Maggie frowned. Don't be bitter, she scolded herself. It was alarming how easy resentment and bitterness and envy could be. Alarming, but perversely satisfying, too.

Another gold-framed picture, one of Maggie and Kelly at Aspen three winters ago, tilted back on Gordon's lawyer desk. Or it had been there. Would Gordon now have cut Maggie out, or turned the photo face down in the bottom drawer of his desk? He was so careful, so meticulous, and such a perfectionist that Maggie envisioned him Xacto-knifing her out and leaving the space blank. To be filled in later with another, more nearly perfect wife? "Well, good luck to her," Michelle would say. "Whichever unlucky woman she might be."

Now Robert Livingston III leaned across the table. He flipped through the papers. Finally satisfied, he turned the packet towards Maggie. "Your copy," he said. "For your records—taxes, social security, and so on. Oh, and a document Gordon's lawyer forwarded to me. Something Gordon wanted you to have."

Robert Livingston sorted through the stack of papers. "Here it is. A spreadsheet that itemizes all your assets, plus your projected income for ten years, along with his suggested budget he thought you might find useful."

Maggie glanced at the document. "So he's giving me a budget telling me how and when to spend my money."

"It's only a suggestion."

Maggie took a deep breath and sat back in her chair.

"Do you have a shredder?" she asked.

Her lawyer nodded. She handed him the spreadsheet. "Then use it!"

"I think he's only trying to be helpful. But, well, okay. Whatever you say." He scrawled SHRED across the spreadsheet and set it aside.

5

He slid a single sheet across the desk. "Your signature, please. Acknowl-edging that you have received the copies."

The lawyer handed Maggie a pen. "Today is?" she asked.

"The 28th," Livingston said. "August 28th," as if she had no idea of the month.

"1998?" Maggie asked, straight-faced, and she thought the lawyer almost smiled when he nodded. "Yes, August 28, 1998." Later, that was all she would remember. "The End" should follow, the way all ordinary, old-fash-ioned stories ended. She should try to remember this, she knew, but instead could only concentrate on a tiny white scar on Livingston's forehead. That, and a suspicious-looking mole. Too much sun. He should have it checked, she thought.

Finally the lawyer glanced at his watch. "Well," he said at last. "This all seems to be in order. If we're lucky the judge will rubber stamp the financial settlement and when we're done the check will be deposited into your account. So, if you're ready, I guess we can go." His eyes met hers. He straightened his bow tie and slipped on a suit coat that covered his suspenders. When she slid her chair back Maggie felt his glance touch her knees, then move quickly up.

"Well, if you're ready," he said.

The elevator sank thirty-three floors in a few seconds, wheezed to a bounce/lift stop, and then bonged a mellow bong. When the doors slid open Maggie stepped forward, clutching her red purse to her chest. Sadness and regret mingled with excitement, but suddenly relief won out and flooded in. Her relief to be free of Gordon and the house and Robert Livingston III; to be free to hit the road to Mexico with her camera.

Maggie tried to visualize her future. She would venture deep into that strange country, driving her red Chevy Blazer. And she would venture deep into herself. She almost floated along the sidewalk, astounded by her possibilities.

CHAPTER 2

Twenty-four hours later, on a Saturday evening in late August, Maggie cruised down Interstate 35, now through the confusion of San Antonio toward the tangle and jumble of Laredo. For the next fifty miles she pushed the Blazer, racing against the sun that faded like a burned-out flare across the wasteland to the west. She had planned to be in Laredo before dark, with time to orient herself in that strange border town. Finding a decent place to spend the night, a clean and safe and comfortable motel, was not something Maggie wanted to attempt in the Laredo darkness. Not alone.

She forced the Blazer to seventy, gripping the wheel tight against the vehicle's high-speed shimmy. But well north of the border the creosote bushes and stunted mesquites to her right and left faded into shadows, and when she reached the edge of town the strip centers and would-be malls and fast-food stops were already bright-lit against the black smear of sky.

Cautiously Maggie picked her way down to the heart of town until she spotted the international bridge and the oversized sign, TO MEXICO. She slowed almost to a stop and glanced to the far end of the bridge, hoping for a hint of what tomorrow might bring.

But now, at night, all she could make out was a line of idling cars and the glare of lights that faded into the cross-border yellow haze.

Tomorrow she would cross the bridge. But now she swung west and moved along a feeder street that followed the curve of the Rio Grande. A series of floodlights cast a shimmer of light and shadow across the ravines and draws that ran at right angles along the river bank. Shadowy figures floated here and there, wafting from dark to light, animating the scene in an ominous, spooky sort of way. Maggie hit the button that locked the Blazer's doors.

A couple of border agents in a green and white van gave her no more than a glance as she eased by. They seemed to be alert to the dark silhouettes that moved quickly between river and road. Maggie imagined the mysterious figures still dripping from the river crossing, secreting caches of drugs or black market goods. Or maybe they were only hurrying home after working all day. Maggie would need to watch her sometimes out-of-control imagination.

She pulled into an Exxon station and topped off the tank until gas overflowed onto the pavement. Without asking, a small Mexican man wiped her windshield with a sloppy rag, then squeegeed it dry. Maggie offered the man a couple of dollars to check the oil and tires, the fan belts and battery for tomorrow's long drive. He shrugged and shook his head. "For you there is no charge." He fiddled with the hood latch a moment, then stopped. Maggie could feel the intensity of his dark eyes. "You headed south," motioning with his head towards the river. He nodded, answering his own question. He touched the bill of his COWBOYS cap. He pulled a stiff red rag from his back pocket and wiped his hands. He wore a striped shirt with the logo of a smiling tiger above his name, Lupe, that was stitched in wavering cursive.

He raised the hood. "These Chebys, they are good," he grunted.

Chebys? Maggie thought. She smiled.

"These older ones. Plenty good."

Lupe leaned under the hood and mumbled something, as if he could communicate with the Blazer in a secret language. He straightened up. "What is this? A '93?"

"1994, I think," Maggie said. Gordon had given it to her for Christmas four years earlier. It was a demonstrator. All of their Houston friends drove Jeeps or Suburbans or Ford Explorers, and Gordon didn't want to be left behind. It seemed that a new SUV for the old wife was the next best thing to a new, younger wife.

"The newer Chebys. Now, they're bad news." Lupe wiped his hands on the red rag again.

8

Bad news, good news. She had the Blazer, for better or worse, and simply had to trust it to carry her safely into Mexico.

But Maggie felt lost, confused, the same way she had felt when Dr. Ramsey, her mother's oncologist in Houston, described the variety of cancer that had eaten away at her mother's body. After his diagnosis the doctor had wiped his hands, slowly, methodically, while he delivered the bad news. Just like Lupe with the red rag, the doctor with white paper towels. The wiping of hands seemed to be a professional mannerism that cut across the classes.

"The new ones," Lupe continued, "they're not so good, not like these older babies. And these, they disappear all the time; these old Chebys, all the time. For parts, mostly." He checked the tension of the belts, pushing each with his thumb. Finally he straightened up and then slammed the hood shut. He wiped the rag across the smudge of his fingerprints. "Yeah, parts for this baby are worth a lot. Any truck stop mechanic can make this engine hum." He grinned. "Even a Mexican. Like me. No problema."

Maggie turned away from Lupe, dug through her purse and fished out a twenty-dollar bill for the gas.

"You travel alone?" Lupe asked. He raised his eyebrows in a way that struck Maggie as betraying more than a passing interest.

"Oh," Maggie said. She wagged her head side to side. Her voice was forced casual. Maggie didn't lie well. "My husband. He's back at the motel. He's not very good with things like cars, you know."

Lupe nodded, gave a little shrug, but Maggie noticed that he stood there eyeing the Blazer as she pulled away. He hadn't turned back to the station when she rounded the next corner and hurried north.

God, Maggie, she thought. If you can't even get through Laredo, Texas, without a panic attack, how in the world will you ever get to Oaxaca? She took a deep breath, trying to shake the fatigue, the tension in her shoulders. She needed a more definite plan, some better purpose than driving south through Mexico with her camera. A fake, that's what she was. A fake and a fraud.

Why didn't she just go back to Houston, rent a small condo on the west side of the city, and get a job? A real one. Put her proceeds from the sale of the house and her share of their investments into a nice safe CD. And Maggie still had most of a small inheritance from her mother. She could be a suburban divorcee. Lots of other women did that. She'd have plenty of company. Come on, Maggie, she thought. Join the real world. You're not a photographer, anyway. Not a real one.

She sped away from the Rio Grande on what had been the main north/south highway before the interstate bullied its way through town. She moved past pawn shops and a crowded car wash. A neon dollar sign flashed from a loan company's window. In a couple of blocks she came upon a strip of small motels—The Sands, The Siesta. She laughed out loud at the Kon-Tiki with its neon hula girl shimmying out front. Yellow plastic signs promised cheap rates. Another advertised XXX movies with free ice and free local calls. A couple of the motels looked okay, and she slowed at their entrances, but sank when she spotted the motley collection of battered pickups and cars nosed in at the rooms. She accelerated on by.

Maggie mentally tallied up her resources, tried to put those dollars into some kind of long-term perspective, but after plodding her way through three or four affordable months in Mexico, things got muddled. Maybe she discounted Gordon's spreadsheet too quickly. She shook her head and whispered, "No, no, no!" She wasn't poor. She wasn't broke. Not rich either, but she wasn't feeble in mind, or for now, in body. Her mother's slow death, the surgery and the horrible scarring had marked Maggie. Her own vulnerability scared her, especially now, when she was on her own. But she would survive somehow.

With a quick glance in the side mirror Maggie whipped the Blazer left and U-turned right in the middle of the block. "Come on Cheby," she said. "We're going first class!"

Just before the international bridge she pulled into the entrance of La Posada Hotel. At the front desk she asked for a room with a river view. "And have room service send up a BLT on whole wheat toast. Go light on the mayo. And a half-carafe of Pinot Noir if you have one from Oregon, a California anything red if you don't."

"No," she said as an afterthought. "Not a half-carafe. Make that a bottle."

The clerk nodded. "Whatever you would like," he said with a slight bow. Maggie tossed her head and tapped her fingernails on the counter. She could be imperious when necessary. In the middle of a hot-tempered negotiation over splitting retirement benefits, Gordon had referred to Maggie as "Her Uppity-ness." So what, she thought. It's all about survival.

The desk clerk hit the bell twice. He handed the key to a stooped man in a faded uniform who slung Maggie's bag over his shoulder and escorted her to the third-floor room.

Later, with the lights off, she pulled the drapes open wide. She had slipped on one of Kelly's too-big Black Sabbath T-shirts and stood there, sipping the wine and staring at the pattern of dim lights across the border. From Maggie's hotel window, Nuevo Laredo didn't appear to be strange at all. They're just folks, she thought. Just like me. Folks trying to make it through this crazy life the best they can. What difference does a muddy river make anyway? Or a little different language?

Maybe it was the shower and the sandwich. Or maybe the wine. But Maggie no longer felt afraid. She had an urge to call Michelle, to let her know she had made it this far and tell her that now she knew she would go on. She needed to hear her friend say, "You bet. You are one good photographer. Now you just go for it."

But Maggie didn't place the call, for Michelle was out of the picture. The now almost ancient camera, an OM1 she had bought from Michelle, was in Maggie's hands. It was discovery time.

CHAPTER 3

Maggie crossed the Rio Grande bridge early Saturday morning. She had followed the *Inmigración* signs down a wide boulevard, and pulled in at a barn-like building set back off of the road. At the immigration center men eyed her—she felt their eyes—and she shamelessly, secretly enjoyed the way their attention heightened her sense of adventure. Now, finally outside of Houston and Texas and, yes, outside of America, Maggie could be her own woman. No more controlling husband or demanding kid or dictating lawyer. She wanted to sing, or twirl around the crowded room in a celebratory dance. Free! At last she was free.

Or maybe Maggie was fooling herself.

The customs officer on the Mexican side, a slender and polite man, shuffled the papers before him with the ease of a Reno croupier. He asked, by rote, a series of questions. What is your destination? How long will you be there? Maggie answered as best she could. She felt relieved when he stamped the visa, made it good for the maximum 180 days. Six months! Oh, yes. She truly was free. For six long months.

Finally, the customs officer pushed his hat back on his head and held the papers out. Maggie tried to take them, but for a moment he held them tight. "Do you travel alone?" he asked.

She took a shallow breath and returned his stare. "Yes," she said. "If it's any of your business—which it isn't—I am traveling alone. I am a professional photographer." He pulled the papers back and glanced at the visa Maggie had earlier filled out. Under occupation she had written "Photographer."

He lifted his dark eyebrows. "But where is your husband?" he seemed to ask. And with another glance he telegraphed a second, silent judgment—or a question—one that Maggie could not quite read.

His eyes moved quickly from passport photo to Maggie and back again before coming to rest on this gringa lady, and languidly cruised up and down. Maggie self-consciously ran her fingers through her hair.

Michelle had talked her into this short haircut, which Maggie could see as practical. But she had balked when Michelle had pushed for tinting her sandy hair red. At forty-six Maggie would accept who she was—no beauty, but slender in her khaki pants and a long-sleeved white blouse that she wore to protect her pale skin from the sun.

The customs agent handed her the papers again—the Mexico car permit and visa, her passport and driver's license, together with various imponderable stamped and stapled-together receipts.

Maggie turned to go, then half-turned back. She hesitated a moment to be sure she had the Mexican's attention, and gave him a quick wink. The wink was not a come-on at all, which would have been silly and contrary to who Maggie now was, who Maggie wanted to be. The wink was simply a way for her to feel once more alive, to feel that Mexico, stretching its sensuous curve to the south, held possibilities for her.

On the dusty south side of the Rio Grande with a TURISTA sticker on the Blazer's windshield, Maggie weaved her way down the crowded boulevard toward the outskirts of Nuevo Laredo. The traffic raced three abreast on the two marked lanes, as if the pickups and step-vans and mostly junker cars were bound together by invisible, stretchable bands, expanding and contracting to always overfill the undulating form of the road.

Maggie rode above the clutter and the clatter, the disorder and confusion. She felt serene, sitting high in the Blazer and headed south. Maggie O'Neill, the queen of the boulevard.

Her self-assurance cracked momentarily when she stopped at a casa de cambio to exchange dollars for pesos. In the middle of the currency conversion Maggie's mind stalled. The indifferent young woman behind the thick plate glass counted the bills too fast, snapping each one with a flourish that became a series of flutters, and then a blur that finally ended with her hand—with its long, green fingernails—pushing a stack of strange bills towards Maggie.

She took the pesos and accepted the teller's count with a nod, with a confident, "Gracias," as if she understood that an honest exchange had taken place. But Maggie had no idea how many pesos she stuffed into her fanny pack. Enough so that she suddenly felt rich. She remembered a bad late-night movie, and now understood how the bank robber must have felt stuffing thick wads of bills into his valise, suddenly rich, but always listening for the wail of sirens in the distance.

At last the red Chevy Blazer reached the toll road at the far end of town, and sped powerfully towards Monterrey. In late summer the desert plants—the creosote bushes, the daggered cacti, the feathery mesquite—appeared tired, and had faded to a stubborn green. Not the green of Houston, not lush, Astroturf green, not watered every day and fertilized by Chem-Spray Saint Augustine grass green. But a green that would not fade completely away; a green that would endure.

Maggie found herself reading the road signs. Speed limit signs and turn-around signs and dangerous curve signs rolled off her tongue in bad, gringa Spanish. She trilled her *r*s, which buzzed the nerve endings of her tongue. Years ago, in college, Maggie had endured four semesters of Spanish classes, ending up able to read the Mexican newspapers that trickled into the library's periodicals room two weeks late. She had spent six weeks one summer in Guadalajara on a cultural exchange program, learning more about the amazing varieties of tequila and the aggressiveness of young Mexican men than about the arts of the country.

But now she felt the language coming back, seeping into her consciousness, words and phrases magically flitting through her mind. It would happen. In a few days, or a few weeks at the most, the language would be no problem.

Maggie found a Linda Ronstadt cassette, *Canciones de mi Padre*, one she had bought especially for the road. It was all in Spanish, a tribute to the singer's Mexican roots, and Maggie followed along as best she could: "Ay, Ay, Ay, Ay, *Las nubes van por el cielo*," she sang, the wind whipping her words out and across the Mexican desert where they rose, she imagined, into the puffs of clouds that slid across the sky.

At Monterrey she tired of the tollway and with glances at the Sanborn's map on the seat beside her, worked her way south down the twists of a

14

narrow rural road. She stopped at a Pemex station to top off the gas tank. A clamber of boys wiped at the windshield with newspapers they dipped in a bucket of dirty water.

Maggie locked the Blazer and ventured into the Dama's room. She crouched and peed, suspended above the seatless porcelain toilet, noting that in the future she should always carry tissue and a small bar of soap in her fanny pack. Not a problem. Simply new rules of the road.

Now away from the grind of the toll road, Maggie stopped by tiny *capillas* that rose out of the crests of hills. These small chapels held all sizes of chalky, sad-eyed saints almost smothered by faded plastic flowers and milagros. Maggie stepped around broken vases, stopped before waxy altars coated with the drippings from hundreds of melted candles.

Travelers stopped here to light candles and offer prayers—insurance against burned-out brakes and slick-tire blowouts and thrown engine rods. The capillas smelled of candles made from rendered hog fat, and they smelled of urine.

Maggie photographed the shrines, on her knees in the gravel of the pull-offs, always watchful, and nonchalantly back in the Blazer when a pickup slowed as it rattled by. She ignored the plastic sacks snagged in the brush at the edge of the road, yellowed and turned brittle by the sun.

Crosses marked the road. Places of death. Sometimes the crosses stood thick as sprouted seedlings, especially on curves and at not-quite-two-lane bridges. Crosses rose at the crests of hills. These *descansos* mostly were simple wooden crosses with faded names—often a Rodriguez or Morales—and dates scrawled in black or red paint. Wrought-iron fences enclosed more elaborate marble monuments.

Maggie stopped every few miles. She picked her way past faded plastic flowers and scattered shards of vases. She photographed the crosses, automatically, without thinking. The strangeness mesmerized her. Maggie the artist—the newly discovered and liberated artist—sensed shape and color, texture and form. Maggie the woman sensed the sadness that hovered over it all; the sadness of absolute loss.

As Maggie moved farther south, the road dropped into a valley, following a nameless, sluggish river from village to village. She left the desert behind and eased past clusters of simple adobe houses and fields of alfalfa and pastures of bony cows. She sighted down rows of corn and beans and squash. The rows stuttered as she sped by.

Fields of chiles glowed red and stretched for miles. Strands of chiles hung drying from porches; chiles lay spread out on clear plastic sheeting; and chiles completely covered tin roofs of sheds.

Always there were people, men on bicycles, men and women in the fields, entire families waiting roadside for the smoke-spewing third-class diesel buses. There were impossible numbers of workers, heading to the fields and from the fields, packed into the beds of straining pickups and swaying in the backs of bob-tail trucks.

In even the smallest pueblos Maggie stopped at the markets. She ignored the eyes that followed her everywhere, and snapped roll after roll of film, capturing pyramids of marble-sized limes and color-of-the-earth potatoes. She focused on flat, hand-woven baskets overflowing with strange herbs, and clay vessels piled with a dozen varieties of beans. The smells overcame her.

The divorce had left Maggie without appetite. Food had lost its appeal. But now the comals of fried tortillas and the griddles of stringy beef and pots of bubbling stews turned her ravenous. She was wary of the food vendors—had heard the stories, had listened to the warnings. The last thing she wanted was to be sick. To die instantly on the curve of a Mexican road did not unduly frighten her, but a wave of dread seeped through Maggie when she thought of being sick, hurting and alone, even with a simple case of the turistas. So she ate her fill of what she could peel, bananas and mangoes and papayas, mottled-skin oranges and bird-pecked apples.

Hesitantly at first, then with a simple question, a nod, and a little sign language when things got sticky, Maggie photographed the proud vendors. For payment she purchased more fruit than she could eat and vegetables she had no way to cook. At the edge of one market she peeled a ripe mango the size of a small melon and devoured it all.

On the outskirts of town she pulled to the side of the road and left her overflowing sack of produce with a puzzled woman who swept the hard-packed dirt between the road and her house. The woman stopped long enough to nod her thanks and to cross herself quickly. Thanks be to God for small miracles, Maggie could almost hear her say. And thanks be to God for large ones, Maggie murmured, as she drove away.

Always there were the churches. Even in the distance, rising from among the smallest bunching of simple adobe houses, the bell towers and spires and crosses reached toward the sky. Maggie the photographer felt drawn to the churches, to their simple geometry and their spare interiors. These were not the churches and cathedrals of the cities, with their gilded profusion, with a splendor that shouted its presence to the heavens. These churches stood simple and unadorned, home for a cherished, glass-boxed saint or two. Places of straight-back wooden pews and stone floors and plastered walls. Places of cool refuge from the dry heat of midday.

In one, a woman on her knees blocked the aisle, and a withered, ragged man missing one leg claimed the front steps. "Nearer my God to Thee," Maggie thought, a refrain from her solid Methodist childhood. "Nearer my God to Thee," a refrain, also, from her father's funeral when she was twelve, and from her mother's memorial service still etched in her mind.

Maggie understood the impulse, the need to be closer to something, to be not completely abandoned and left alone.

In the village of La Ascensión, on the back road between Monterrey to Matehuala—the small city where Maggie planned to spend the night—she spent most of two hours wandering with her camera. She found piglets wallowing in the dirt street, and a barefoot girl of six or so who toted a sloshing pot of water on her shoulder. She took several shots of a burro in the mottled shade of a mesquite tree, sway-backed with the weight of firewood gathered from the nearby hills. A woman of indeterminable age flattened corn tortillas in a homemade wooden press. Always the bougainvilleas climbed, billowing with purple and red and salmon colors, escaping up the crumbling walls.

Maggie bought a Coke from a corner tienda and rested on an ornate wrought iron bench in the zócalo, the small park that fronted the church of San Augustín. No one bothered her, although small children pointed at the strange gringa from their mothers' arms.

Maggie's friend, Michelle, had warned her of Mexico, the danger of traveling there alone. Maggie had heard the stories of highway bandits and purse snatchers and puzzled over newspaper accounts of Americans who had simply disappeared.

Maggie took Michelle's words seriously, for her friend was no conservative Houston alarmist, afraid to venture out of her gated community. Michelle freelanced as a photographer, mostly for the *Houston Chronicle*, rushing off to fires and the bloody splatter of car wrecks and gang wars.

Once a year Michelle taught a short course in advanced photo journalism at the local museum, a course that Maggie had taken as a diversion from her mother's chemo sessions, and as an escape from a withdrawn, soon-to-be ex-husband.

But the photography course had opened Maggie up to the possibilities of the medium, and led to a quick sequence of other classes. Before long Maggie made her commitment—the purchase of the pricey, even if used, Olympus, and now she felt lost without it.

Michelle had been the key—Maggie was drawn to her mentor's independence, the feistiness and doggedness that allowed her to compete and succeed—a black woman in a white man's world.

After one of their photography classes, Michelle had wanted a glass of wine. "I need a buzz all the way down to my toes," she told Maggie, and the two of them slipped over to the darkness of the Plaza Hotel bar, just off of South Main, not far from the Contemporary Museum.

Right away Maggie spilled out her idea about going to Mexico, emphasizing the money she could save, the anticipated freedom, all of those quaint and colorful scenes that she imagined.

"Mexico, huh?" Michelle said. "So you're going to Mexico. But where? Now Mexico, it's a big-ass place, girlfriend. Where about you gonna go?"

Maggie laughed. She shook her head. "Uhmm. Well, San Miguel de Allende first, then maybe Oaxaca. Somewhere exotic, for sure."

"Oaxaca," Michelle said. "Yeah. Exotic is good. You need something exotic. Find you a bullfighter down there, maybe." Michelle appeared to drift off for a moment, deep into her own fantasy of Mexico.

"No bullfighter, Michelle. This isn't about men. This trip is about me, Maggie O'Neill. Without a man."

Michelle shook her head, her dreadlocks glistening in the neon glow of the bar. "Oaxaca, Mexico. I like the way that sounds." She hesitated a moment, worried looking, then with a grin raised her wine glass in a toast. "Whoo-ee! You are something else, girl."

Suddenly Michelle leaned forward, conspiratorially. "Now I know this dude," she said. "And he knows Mexico. He's done business there." She rolled her eyes. "Too much business." Michelle laughed, poked Maggie's arm with her finger. "He's a hunk besides. Listen, girl, I tell him to go with you, and he's packed, he's with you, right up front in that Jeep of yours."

"A Blazer," Maggie said. "And no to the hunk!"

"Whatever. Anyway he owes me one. More than one. It wasn't for me, that boy, he'd be coolin' it in Huntsville for twenty some-odd years."

Michelle took a long drink. "Praise the Lord for the grape," she said with a laugh and leaned close once more. "Now, no shit, Maggie," Michelle

18

said. She touched Maggie's arm for emphasis. Her smooth black fingers and purple fingernails startled Maggie for a moment. "You watch your sweet ass down there. Take no chances. You hear?"

Michelle was Maggie's treasure, the only person she left behind who came close to understanding her. "You go with me," Maggie told her friend, and she meant it. But Michelle just laughed, and shook her head.

Maggie had heard her friend's warnings, and until now had taken them seriously. But in places such as this, the village of *La Ascensión*, danger seemed ludicrous. For in Mexico there seemed no way to be alone. Everywhere Maggie stopped, people mysteriously appeared. They stepped from behind trees or suddenly materialized, squatting in the shade of walls. They rose from picking beans in a field or came to life next to a pile of stones.

The men mostly ignored her. The women watched her with open curiosity, but never, so far, had she felt the least hostility or resentment. "Maggie," Michelle would say. "You're too easy, a number-one romantic."

But Matehuala was a different story. Maggie had poked around La Ascensión too long and pulled into that stopover town just after dark, although she had promised herself, and promised Michelle, that she wouldn't drive that late. All of the guide books preached against driving after dark, and now Maggie knew why. For the last few kilometers into Matehuala she had hurried on, hitting her lights back and forth, dim and bright, easing past men bicycling home in the dark on the shoulder-less roads, and braking hard when she came upon a burro-drawn wagon. Her hands ached from gripping the wheel.

Trucks and buses crowded behind Maggie's Blazer and flashed their lights, hurrying on to their stop in Matehuala, impatient to roar around the cautious gringa.

Matehuala apparently existed because it lay halfway between Monterrey and San Luis Potosí. Over the years it had grown to be the only decent— somewhat decent—stopover in the high desert, an artificial, man-made oasis of truck stops and cheap motels, of roadside vendors with stacks of copper pots and black pottery, and trucks headed north that overflowed with oranges. Pemex stations held lines of cars and trucks that idled constantly. Their exhaust mixed with smoke from the open fires of taco and carne asada stands, rising to blend with the clouds of dust that hovered above the unpaved side streets. After dark Matehuala took on a feeling of gloom that could dishearten weary travelers.

In the heart of town Maggie found a motel, the Isla de Palmas, set back from the road. Its 1950s neon sign of palm trees shimmered against the night sky. She asked the indifferent clerk to show her a room. It passed Maggie's sniff test, the room smelling of sun-dried sheets and the vague remnants of something pleasant enough, something that at first she couldn't quite name. Then it came to her. Damn! After-shave lotion. Would she never get away from men?

In the tiny bathroom the lavatory faucet dripped, staining a rusty streak down to the drain. But there was a wrapped bar of soap, and two thin towels hung over the edge of the bathtub.

The clerk turned the television set on and maneuvered the rabbit ears until some wavy lines moved in and out of focus. He shrugged with a slight bow and moved towards the door.

The room had baked, shut tight all day. And suddenly Maggie gave a gasp. She felt as if she might suffocate, and panicked for a moment. She pointed to the air conditioner stuck in the concrete block wall. "It's okay?" she asked in desperate English. "It works?"

The clerk nodded, said something that Maggie couldn't catch, words that sounded like reverential praise for the machine in the wall. He flipped a switch and the AC jerked to life with a clang and then a roar. But in a few moments it belched cool air.

Maggie handed the clerk a few random coins and stood at the open door as he left. A swimming pool across the way broke up an expanse of pea gravel. There were a few sun-yellowed plastic chairs scattered around the edge. In the center of the pool a cherub peed water in a continuous stream. Maggie wouldn't swim, but she did picture herself later, relaxing by the pool for a few minutes before bedtime.

To her right, back up the driveway, she studied the bright-lit motel restaurant. Not too promising. But she mentally inventoried the provisions in the Blazer—a half jar of dry-roasted peanuts, a piece of rubbery cheddar cheese, and a small box of raisins. Who could tell? The restaurant might surprise her. She closed and locked the door—just a pushbutton in the door-knob, no chain, no deadbolt.

Maggie sagged and sank down on the edge of the bed. The mattress scrunched as if it were filled with straw, but would have to do. This was it for the night. Maggie knew she could go no farther.

There was hot water, warm water really, but plenty of pressure, and

Maggie showered, careful not to let even a drop of water pass her lips. She thought about whales, the way they must take gigantic breaths before they dive deep. She did that, felt herself become wonderfully whale-like. She took huge breaths before leaning her head under the shower, and held those breaths until her lungs ached. Then, with a jerk of her head she exploded, spewing out the stale air. She wiped her lips with the end of a towel.

From her soft suitcase she dug out fresh underwear, then clean khaki pants and a shirt. It was amazing what a shower could do. That, and a change of clothes—even if they were a little wrinkled.

In the restaurant a waiter wearing an oversized maroon jacket greeted her with a formal bow. He led her to a table with four *Estado de San Luis Potosí* placemats, and gathered up three of them. He pulled out her chair and popped a stiff white napkin open before spreading it across her lap. He pointed above, to where a television set hung suspended from the ceiling. "This table," he said. "It is the very best."

Maggie nodded her thanks, and looked up. Some game show was on, the emcee assisted by a well-endowed woman who wore a blonde wig and a shimmering, low-cut dress. The audience howled and shrieked. The woman jiggled and cavorted. A job I will mark off my list of possibilities, Maggie thought. But she smiled, suddenly open to so many possibilities.

The menu held little promise, but she ordered the beef steak Tampiqueña, which the waiter, Jesús on his name tag, heartily recommended. She asked about wine, and Jesús looked puzzled, glancing back towards the kitchen as if he might try to conjure a bottle from somewhere. Maggie let him off the hook by ordering a Dos Equis, and he nodded, visibly much relieved.

For a few minutes she was alone in the restaurant. From her table she caught glimpses of the comings and goings in the adjacent motel office, heard men joke and laugh and bargain for better rates. Men did that. In any language, including Spanish, this halfway foreign language, men seemed to carry invisible powers that extended out, overpowering everything around them. Maybe that's why they start wars, Maggie thought. Those invisible extensions always bumping and banging around, the men oblivious to the damage they are doing.

With a slight bow Jesús delivered a bowl of crisp-fried tostadas, thick and heavy with the taste of lard, and a bowl of sauce. Maggie nibbled, sipped the beer.

A trio of men burst into the room, stout men with deep, rich voices and aggressive gestures. They wore western straw hats and exotic reptile-skin boots, starched white shirts and stiff, creased jeans. It seemed to Maggie that the restaurant might not hold these men, for they confirmed what she had just conjectured. Maggie watched, closing her eyes slightly, hoping that she might in this way bring into focus those invisible power fields that men possessed.

When the three of them spotted Maggie, they quickly lifted their hats in unison, almost comically, and she smiled to herself. They took a table next to Maggie—the next best table in the place—and positioned the chairs so that all three of them faced the television.

Maggie watched from the corner of her eye. These men appeared to be regulars, most likely traveling businessmen of some sort, for Jesús, without asking, brought three dark bottles of Bohemia beer to the table along with the menus. The older man—not that old, Maggie observed—stood out, with his trimmed moustache and smooth skin and straight combed-back hair. She noted the slight paunch that overhung his cowhide belt when he moved to the television set. There, rising on the toes of his boots, he flipped the channels, stopping on a boxing match. Maggie read his name, "Carlos," tooled in block letters on the back of his belt.

When Carlos turned back to his table one of his companions gestured with his head, moved it just ever so slightly, and cut his eyes towards Maggie. Carlos stopped abruptly and turned to the gringa woman. He gave a slight bow and in passable English told her he was sorry. "Perhaps it is your wish to watch the other channel," he said. "If you want I will return it. No?"

Maggie smiled and shook her head.

"Thank you very much," Carlos said with another bow, and joined his friends. They nodded their approval.

I could get used to this, Maggie thought. All of this bowing and scraping, the old-fashioned gentility, touched her. Being a gringa lady in Mexico might have some advantages she hadn't counted on. Perhaps she would grow up and become a fairy princess after all, for when she was small her daddy had called her his fairy princess. And from somewhere deep she felt a sadness start to rise in her throat. I'm just tired, she thought. It's okay.

She felt a generation of feminists looking over her shoulder, wagging their disapproving fingers at her, but she dismissed them with a shake of her head and a generous swallow of beer.

With a flourish Jesús placed a platter of food before her, turning it until he gave a nod of satisfaction. With a lilting string of quick-fire words he pointed out the pounded-thin steak grilled with onions and peppers, the bowl of soupy beans, and an enchilada stuffed with white cheese. Slices of avocado topped it all. A napkin-covered basket held a stack of thick and chewy corn tortillas. Enough food for three Maggies.

Jesús brought her a saucer of lime quarters. "For the *bifstek*," he said, making an imaginary lime-squeeze over the platter. With a flourish he placed another Dos Equis beside her half-finished one. "Compliments of the Señor," he said, motioning to the other table.

Carlos half-rose from his chair, gave an exaggerated sweep of his arm, and nodded his head.

Oh, God, Maggie thought. What have I done now? Quickly she figured that to refuse the beer would be some sort of insult, so she smiled at Carlos. "Gracias," she said softly, and Carlos broke into a grateful flurry of nods.

Okay, Maggie, she told herself. New rules. If this were the Plaza Hotel bar and Michelle was next to me we would have some fun—if that's what we wanted. Or Michelle would in a Houston minute tell an over-aggressive man where he could go and what he could do.

But this was different, and Maggie didn't understand the signals, the foreign protocol for all of this man/woman interaction.

She seriously attacked the plate of food, pausing only to squeeze fresh lime juice over the steak, then a little down the narrow neck of her beer. The ever-watchful Jesús nodded his approval.

The food was wonderful, the cheese white and creamy, the steak a little stringy, but loaded with straight-off-the-range flavors she had never tasted. The second cold Dos Equis eased through her, finally unlocking the tension and fatigue from the long day, dissipating the strangeness of being there alone. A little buzz isn't bad, Maggie reasoned. When you've traveled as far as I have, you deserve whatever buzzes life affords.

With a pose of sureness Maggie signed the check and left. She didn't even glance at the three men, concentrating, over-dramatically she suspected, on her shoulder bag, as she fished for her room key.

Outside, the desert air had cooled and a slight breeze rattled through the palms. Most of the rooms were taken now, cars and trucks crowded into all of the spaces out front, and lights from the rooms threw bright patches of white onto the gravel drive.

Outside Maggie's room the Blazer glowed in the night, an easy target for a break-in, and she decided to bring her camera in. Thieves could have the rest, for all she cared.

When she closed the door to the room, the air conditioner popped on and roared, drowning out the sounds from the highway, along with whatever comings and goings might take place outside the room. But in an hour or so the room cooled and the wall unit stopped with a clunk.

Maggie found herself moving in and out of a light sleep. The dry foam cubes of the pillow crunched when she stirred. Once she woke from a dream, and lifted her head to better hear what seemed to be a scratching at the door. Carlos? She wondered. Please God, not Carlos. She tiptoed to the door and pushed the center button of the knob hard—something she knew she had done earlier. But better to be overly cautious.

She waited at the window and had an urge to wind it open. Maggie wanted to hear the breeze sweep through the oasis of palm trees. She wanted to feel the coolness of the night breeze on her skin.

But there was the scratching once again, and now she could tell that it came from below, at the bottom of the door. She pulled back the curtain just enough to see outside and at that moment a startled rat scampered away from the door and toward the pool.

Now she could sleep again, but for a while she didn't. Maggie wondered what Carlos and his friends had said about her when she left the restaurant. They would have seen a woman, middle-aged, but still attractive. A woman who appeared to know what she was about. A classy woman from America.

They couldn't have known the real Maggie, a woman already weary of the road, a woman with tears and loneliness dammed up not far behind her eyes.

They might have figured she was a mother, for weren't all women in Mexico mothers? And they would have been right. But she didn't wish Kelly was here with her, nor did she honestly wish that he would be waiting for her at the end of this trip, wherever that might be. She was a mother, and not a bad one. But at twenty-four Kelly needed his freedom, his independence. And she needed hers, too.

Maggie wished that in the restaurant she had stood up and announced to the three men, "I know what you're thinking, but you're wrong. I am not just another ordinary woman. I am a photographer, a professional photographer. I am an artist. Tomorrow I am going to San Miguel de Allende, to get on with my business." That sounded much more confident than Maggie felt.

She should have brought her Olympus to the restaurant and placed it on the table. Then they might have known, or wondered, at least. Everything was confusing. And she was so tired.

But her mind would not let her rest. The men's eyes must have followed her across the restaurant. Or maybe they weren't interested in forty-something women. How could she know what men wanted? Why did she still care?

What would they think about a woman who at midnight, in Room 116 of the Isla de Palmas Motel, lay awake and listened? What would they think about a woman who was not at all afraid to hear a soft scratching at her door?

CHAPTER 4

San Miguel de Allende appeared to be a treasure. Houston party talk almost always held stories of this small city in the upslope of Mexico's Sierra Madre mountains. Maggie's doctor, Dr. Ramsey, confirmed the stories when she stopped in for a pre-trip checkup and a "Health Tips for Foreign Travel" brochure he had developed after being a part of Doctors Without Borders for a few months back in the 70s. "San Miguel's a mix," he said, "and some folks say it's not the real Mexico." He shrugged and handed Maggie a prescription for use only in case of a severe turista attack. "But I think you'll love it, especially for a few days stopover."

He also gave her the name of a doctor he knew in Oaxaca. "Arturo Reyes," he said. "Internal medicine. A bright fellow. A little moody. Latin through and through. We went through residency in Dallas together." He shuffled through his desk drawer and scribbled Arturo Reyes's name and number on the back of a prescription pad. "Give him a call if you get down there. But I have a feeling you won't get past San Miguel."

Well, Maggie would see. She planned to stay in San Miguel a day or two and check the place out. Oaxaca was still a long drive to the south, but Maggie felt no need to hurry.

By mid-afternoon on Monday she eased the Blazer down a narrow street that opened up into the center of town and immediately knew that Dr. Ramsey had been right. San Miguel was genuinely quaint—the cobblestone streets, the lovely, shaded plaza, the profusion of colors that startled and overwhelmed. Right away Maggie felt energized by the magic of the place.

For a couple of hours she wandered the streets, stunned by the glow that shimmered from the houses and the walls that often hid them. Inside a tiny courtyard she devoured a late lunch of *caldo Xochitl* with a side dish of aromatic rice and sauteed nopalitos. She sipped on a mix of melon and papaya juices served in a pale green hand-blown glass.

A hotel around the corner was ridiculously inexpensive. Her third-floor room opened out onto a portal that overlooked the cathedral and distant hills. That evening, just at sundown, she shot an entire roll of slide film while the sun worked its color show across the town. "Okay, Maggie," she whispered with a shake of her head. "Enough sunsets."

The next day she explored, nodding at the tourists who roamed the streets. She wandered away from the center of town, away from the plaza, and found the market. She followed the spillover of stalls that meandered down a steep hill, stepping around stacks of bold Talavera pottery and sweeps of silver jewelry laid out on blankets. Hundreds of handmade sandals hung from strands of rope and stacks of straw hats and copper pots gleamed in the sun. A man shined the copper vessels, rubbing the hammered surfaces with lime halves and a sprinkling of coarse salt.

The shops were stuffed with leather bags and Guatemalan fabrics. Maggie tried on a wide-brimmed straw hat trimmed with a hand-woven band. She loved it. It would protect her from the sun, she rationalized, and she wore it out into the brightness of the street.

Art galleries held a mix of paintings—ancient churches, the ever-present bougainvillea, and the market's profusion of fruits and flowers.

In one gallery, with Santa Barbara, Beverly Hills, and Santa Fe stylishly painted on the glass door, Maggie found one wall lined with pricey photographs. They were finely done, technically without fault, but they all covered familiar territory—the churches, the colorful and worn doors, the flowers, the markets. Maggie found herself disheartened, but also reassured that her photographs were as good as these. At least some of them. Still so much for her to see, to photograph.

As the days in San Miguel moved on, Maggie worked with the Olympus in her dreams. She dreamed in color—soft yellow and daring gold, turquoise and lavender and rose. She dreamed all shades of the Guanajuato earth, together with the tints of sunrise and sunset, and the pure azure of the midday Mexican sky.

On the fourth day there, Maggie stopped by a camera shop and left her rolls of film. She picked them up on Sunday afternoon and hurried back to her room, relieved to be out of the glare of the sun. She set up her projector and clicked through the slides, trying to make sense of the rudimentary log she had kept, although now such abbreviations such as "T'pan mkt. and hrd. of gates & chrch w/black St." made little sense.

As the slides flashed before her, Maggie could see patterns emerge. Churches held a major attraction, with markets a close second. Then came photos of children and animals, and then old men. Maggie confessed to a weakness for old Mexican men. Early on she had tired of roadside capillas and car wreck descansos, but not before she had several dozen shots of those. Then there were the walls—peeling walls and crumbling walls. Walls of all colors. And doors. Painted doors and weathered doors; doors with ornate hardware and doors with crosses. Then sunsets and sunrises. Processions and parades. Saints in glass boxes (too much reflection off the glass, she noted). Seated saints and standing saints. Mostly sad saints. A dozen slides of the Virgin of Guadalupe with her roses. And always Jesus, sad-eyed, mournful, and bleeding.

"Jesus H. Christ," Maggie murmured and laughed in spite of her mood. She felt as if a black claw had gripped her heart. Almost two hundred slides. What would she do with two hundred slides? Slides that seemed to reflect nothing more than the disorder and randomness of her journey, and of her life.

Maggie's eyes raced around the room, taking in the few hangers of mostly white blouses and khaki pants in the closet, a pair of hiking boots next to the chair. The stuff in the bathroom she could cram into a bag in a minute. The camera and slide projector, and two open shelves of underwear and socks. And the slides. She would leave the slides.

Two trips down the stairs. Pay the bill, and adios San Miguel. Adios Mexico, with your foul water and tainted food and diesel fumes and loco drivers. Adios Mexico, with your macho men and obsequious waiters and shifty-eyed beggars and slick-fingered street urchins.

It was getting late, but she could make Matehuala before 8:00. Laredo the next day. Back in Texas she could drive late into the night if she had to. And then? Maggie felt Michelle's heavy presence in the room. Michelle with her hands on her hips, her dreadlocks swaying from side to side. "Sure," Michelle scolded. "We sure do need another dee-vorced, middle-aged woman back in Houston. Maybe you could substitute teach, yeah, junior high art classes. Ooo-eee. Yes, ma'am Miss Maggie. That sure would beat being down there in that bad old Mexico, with all them macho men making eyes at you. And nothing to do but take those pictures. How boring. All day, every day." Then this imagined Michelle started singing. "Go where you want to go, do what you want to do."

"Okay, Michelle, okay," Maggie, in spite of her dark mood, laughed. "That's enough. I get your point."

Maggie did get the point, and in a few minutes was back down on the streets of San Miguel with her camera. She would have these down times. But who wouldn't? Persevere, she told herself. And ease up. Don't be so hard on yourself. She felt Michelle nod her head in agreement.

A couple of blocks north of the plaza on Hidalgo Maggie stepped into the Restaurant Bugambilia. The place overflowed with pots of giant tropical plants, and cages of exotic birds that sang and squawked hung everywhere.

A margarita reinforced Maggie's new resolve. She sipped it, not so slowly, and ordered one more, not wanting the euphoric lift to wear off, afraid of revisiting her black moments in the hotel. She ordered chiles en nogadas sprinkled with pomegranate seeds and slowly felt her strength return.

For a long time she sat in the courtyard and toyed with the stems of the chiles. With one she drew pictures in the remnants of the sauce still smeared across her platter. Maybe the answer for Maggie would suddenly appear before her. Greater miracles than that happened in Mexico all the time. She drew small rectangles in the walnut sauce, picture frames she filled with hills and rivers and stick-legged animals and church towers.

"Ah, another artist, I see." A man's voice. He stood just behind her. Maggie could feel him at her shoulder.

Maggie looked up. Annoyed and embarrassed, she scratched across her plate with a fork, obliterating the crude drawings.

"Not my medium," she said. "Walnut sauce is not what I usually work in."

The man laughed. Without asking he slid into the chair across from Maggie. His hair was thin, the silver strands combed straight back. The skin on his forehead and on the back of his hands had dark splotches here and there. But he was trim and dressed impeccably in a cream-colored silk suit.

Maggie stared at his cufflinks—silver winged horses—that glittered against the pale pink of his shirt.

"Alexander Braun," he said. He didn't extend his hand. "B-r-a-u-n," he spelled it, and Maggie tried to place his accent. British? Faux British? Old Boston?

Maggie nodded.

"And you are?" He opened his hand palm up, as if he were offering something to her. Or, as if he wanted something. Maggie wasn't sure which.

"Maggie," she said.

"That's all?"

Maggie shrugged. Alexander Braun looked harmless enough. But a seventy-something man could be nothing but an irritation. She had an urge to tell him to get lost, but she kept quiet. "You're too quick to say no," she heard Michelle say. Patience, Maggie, she told herself.

"You've been here in San Miguel since Monday," he said. Almost a week now. I was at my usual bench on the plaza. You drive a red . . . what is it? Not a car and not a truck. A 'cruck,' I guess." He gave an amused chuckle, obviously pleased with himself.

Maggie started to say something, but he lifted his hand to cut her off. "Don't worry. I'm not a mad stalker of some sort. I go to the plaza every day during siesta, when the tourists have thinned out, when they are back at their hotels sorting through their mounds of plunder."

Maggie guessed that Alexander Braun might be San Miguel's expatriate eccentric, probably just lonely. She knew she should be decent. Maggie relaxed back in her chair and motioned to her margarita. "Would you like something to drink?"

He glanced at his watch and nodded. "It is after four. In fact, this happens to be my time for drinks. Not a margarita, however." He gave a little frown and turned to the waiter and lifted his finger. The waiter nodded and in less than a minute Alexander was sipping from a shot glass of Irish whisky. "Marvelous service here," he said softly, with a sigh. "I will miss this."

"Are you leaving?" Maggie asked. "Going back to . . . ?"

He shook his head. "Leaving, yes. But that's not important." Then he leaned across the table, and pointed towards the camera on the table. "You are a photographer," he said. "I have seen you every day. You carry that camera, an expensive Olympus, the mark of a professional."

Maggie felt herself flush. "I work at it," she said. "I take my work seriously."

"Then why, for God's sake, do you waste your time here?" He took a deep breath. "In San Miguel? If every building, every church, every wall and door and basket of fruit that has been photographed in this place suddenly disappeared, you and I would be sitting here alone, on a desolate hill." Alexander shook his head. Then he looked at Maggie as if he wanted to say more, something he couldn't find the words for.

"But it's lovely here," Maggie said, and in her mind she saw the photographs she had taken those past few days. They swirled before her, as if fast-forwarded through the lens of her memory. Churches, markets, flowers, walls, doors, sunsets, and on and on. Then she felt herself go flat, in the same way she had sunk in her hotel room when she viewed the slides.

But Maggie caught herself. This was absurd. It was one thing to listen to Michelle pour out her version of life as it should be lived over drinks in a Houston bar. But this? Maggie seriously listening to an old misfit of a fart, a busybody with nothing better to do than be cranky and cynical? Get a grip, she told herself.

"Okay, Mr. Braun," she said.

"Alexander. Please."

"Okay, Alexander. Just where would you suggest that a photographer, such as myself, should go?"

"Not far, my dear Miss Maggie. Not far." He tossed back the last of his whisky. He smiled, and cocked his head to one side. His face seemed no more than a transparent sheath of splotchy skin, the frail covering for his skull. He tapped his chest with a pale, skinny finger. "No, not far at all."

"Oh, that's easy to say." Maggie twirled her finger in the air and gave a rising whistle. "That's so woo-woo. So simple. Just find your inner self, Maggie. The answer is here." She touched her chest. "Right here. Yeah, sure it is."

She pushed back in her chair and motioned for the check. "Get me out of here," she murmured under her breath.

Alexander shrugged. "You don't have to listen."

Maggie stopped, her hands resting on the edge of the table. She waited.

Alexander's voice was low, intense. "Go to *La Casa Azul*, Frida Kahlo's house in Coyoacan. See what she painted. Is Frida Kahlo, as you so quaintly put it, woo-woo? Hardly." He leaned forward again. "She touched her pain, my dear." His eyes now sparkled, flashed just for a moment. "Beneath the parrots and the fruit and the flowers, my hot-headed Miss Maggie, Frida

Kahlo, like all true artists, painted her pain." He sighed once more. "Good art can be unsettling."

"Well," he said. "I have imposed myself on you long enough." He checked his watch again and dropped a few pesos on the table. "It's moving towards five. My time for serious drinks. Much too serious for public places." He rose and gave a slight, gentlemanly bow. His eyes met Maggie's. "I would give anything—anything—to be twenty years younger." He held his gaze steady for a few moments, then turned and was gone.

Maggie sat quietly. The waiter took her pesos for the bill and brought Maggie the change. He stood there for a moment, until Maggie looked up.

"The señor," he said, motioning towards the chair where Alexander Braun had sat. "He is famous in all the world, I believe. They say that he writes music so pure that only the angels are allowed to listen." He shrugged. "But who can know? That is only what they say."

Maggie nodded.

"Now you pay attention," Michelle would say. "Your luck has just changed."

But Maggie didn't believe in luck, and she distrusted chance and fate, for they had worked against her in the past.

For Michelle it was different. Fate and chance were her allies. She believed in signs, that they would guide her through the careen and screech of that grand accident that we call life. "So pay attention, girl."

"I do pay attention," Maggie whispered back to her phantom friend. "I paid attention to the mechanic at the Exxon station in Laredo, and to the customs official at the border. And what about Carlos, at the restaurant in Matehuala, who was not the rat that scratched at my door? None of that mattered, Michelle. Nothing happened. Can't you see?"

"Trust the fates, Maggie."

"Okay, okay. But Alexander Braun? You're trying to tell me to trust him? Another pompous man trying to control my life?"

"But he told you something, Maggie. Those other jerks, they just gave you the eye, the old once over. Big egos and little pricks. Trying to get in your panties. Alexander Braun, now he's different."

"He thought I was attractive," Maggie said, defensively. But Michelle was no longer there. "Michelle! Listen to me! He thought I was attractive."

The waiter hurried over to her table with a confused look. He gave a small bow.

CHAPTER 4

Maggie glanced up. A smile, more than a smile, a glow spread across her face. Fate can't be all bad, she thought.

She would take one small chance and go to Coyoacan.

CHAPTER 5

Gordon would never have driven into Mexico City. And he would have forbidden Maggie to even consider it. "Ha!" Maggie said out loud. She would show him. Better off in the Blazer than in a taxi, Maggie figured. For by now she had seen the taxis in action, the way they seemed to rely for safety solely on the little statuettes of saints firmly affixed to their dashboards. And taxis, she knew, didn't always take their passengers where they wished to go. Instead they carried a scary percentage to dark and deserted side streets, delivering their passengers into the hands of henchmen who relieved them of their valuables, if not their lives. No thank you. Maggie would take her chances in the Blazer.

Just inside the northern edge of Mexico City she pulled into a Pemex for gas, and for a few minutes to collect herself. She checked her map. With her finger she traced the major freeway south, on past the center of the city toward the general vicinity of Coyoacan, where she would find Frida Kahlo's Casa Azul. On the map COYOACAN was stenciled in large blue letters across the jumble of streets, and Maggie pointed her finger there, as if her finger held a magical homing power that would lead her to that place.

She eased the Blazer forward, to the apron of the pavement, waiting for her chance to accelerate into the spin of traffic.

Driving almost this far down from San Miguel had been easy. Maggie's only worry had been the dense cloud of smog that she spotted from miles back, a seemingly solid shadow that hovered over the wide valley ahead of her. But once here the smog wasn't all that bad. It hid the city's immensity and congestion, the endless unfolding of territory that would have been visible and intimidating on a clearer day.

But the smog did lend a dreariness to the city, the cars and trucks hurtling by on the freeway next to the Pemex station emerged ghost-like and rattled and roared by only to disappear once again a quarter of a mile down the highway.

While she waited, for courage she supposed, Maggie devoured a Bimbo bakery sweet roll and immediately felt a sugar rush coming on. She wiped her hands on a Handi-Wipe and eased even closer to the edge of the freeway, hoping that some oncoming car might slow to allow her in.

Finally, she spotted a gap in the rush of traffic and floor-boarded the Blazer. The tires kicked and spewed gravel until they found traction and Maggie bolted south, ignoring the flashing headlights of a truck that suddenly loomed on her rear bumper.

After a few minutes she felt secure enough to whip around a rusted-out Ford that limped along ahead of her. If Michelle were beside her she would be bouncing up and down, urging Maggie on. "Hey," Maggie said to her absent friend, "Mexico City's no worse than Houston. The same game, same rules, mostly take what you can when you get the chance."

Well, Maggie could play that game. She touched her brakes when she came up behind a VW bus with expired California tags and flashed her lights and punched the horn. She jerked the Blazer to the left and hit the gas, picking a gap between the on-racing cars, claiming her territory in the fast, left-hand lane. Cars honked. More lights flashed. Maggie raised her fist, shook it defiantly in the air, and sped on with a grim smile on her face.

Finally she spotted the Coyoacan exit ahead and made her way over, lane by lane, to descend into the whirl and churn of a traffic circle. She looped the Blazer around a couple of times, trapped on the inside lane, before finally spinning out onto a street that led to the east.

Now, drained of energy, she poked along, past a park with towering, small-leafed trees and black iron benches. At midday this part of the city radiated a slow and gracious demeanor. The streets turned from concrete and asphalt to worn-smooth cobblestones. On either side stately homes rose from behind the richly splashed walls. In the park young girls strolled arm in arm under the stern watch of bigger-than-life statues of generals and governors, their hard marble dignity offset by the streaky splatter of pigeon droppings. Vendors pushed carts heavy with ice cream bars and raspados.

Maggie pulled the Blazer to the curb and sat there with the engine idling. I could stay here, she thought. I could live here. A tiny carriage house or a garage apartment was all she would need. Markets were on every street corner. She would sell the Blazer and walk or take the bus. She would photograph the city, the colors, the people, the flowers.

The anonymity of the neighborhood appealed to her. She would never return to Texas. She would contact Kelly and he would come twice a year for visits. That would be enough. She would let Michelle know, but this dignified neighborhood would be too sedate for her. Michelle would never leave the drama of Houston.

Except for her son and her best friend, Maggie would sever all ties and convert her dollars to pesos. She would get a permanent residency permit so she would never again endure that drive to and from the border in order to renew her visa.

In the park she took her chances by devouring a steaming ear of corn slathered in butter and sprinkled with red chili. She realized that her dreaming about living here in Coyoacan was nothing new. She had done the same thing vacationing here and there when life with Gordon still seemed to hold promise. In Santa Fe and Flagstaff and even San Francisco, she remembered thinking, "I could live here," leaving Gordon in the hotel bar and wandering the streets alone, checking out real estate office windows with their overblown ads for fixer-up houses. Now she knew that those dreams of hers weren't about places, but about fresh starts. Alone.

And now she was truly alone. On to Casa Azul.

Alexander Braun, she thought, this had better be worth it. For Maggie knew that Frida Kahlo recently had begun to become ubiquitous in the States, where her image stared solemnly from T-shirts and museum-shop postcards and posters. Frida had been reduced to just another image appropriated to make a few people a lot of bucks. The fiery Mexican artist had been consumed and by now was well on her way to being discarded as a commercial icon.

But here, inside the adobe walls of Casa Azul, Frida Kahlo reclaimed her flesh and blood for Maggie. In the artist's bedroom an unfinished portrait of

Leon Trotsky still leaned on an easel. On Frida's bed Maggie studied one of the plaster corsets that her injury from a streetcar collision had forced her to wear. This one she had decorated, painted with flowers and birds. She read that Frida had suffered in this corset and in twenty-seven others.

In a self-portrait, one corset, made of steel, encircled Frida, her spine the broken shaft of a fluted column. In another painting Frida was naked except for the steel corset and a swirl of cloth draped around her loins. In another, Frida stoic with a desert behind her and a dozen nails piercing her body. Then a bleeding, unconscious Frida with a blood-splattered man standing over her, a knife in his hand. Another, Frida seated, her legs exposed. A stitched cut curved up the inside of her leg. Maggie moved on and found Frida headless, then footless, then split open.

What is this? Maggie wondered. She felt unsettled in the presence of these paintings. What did they mean? All of this—what? Self-disclosure? Exhibitionism? Pure narcissism? Self-pity? Anger? Intimacy?

Maggie picked up a brochure from a rack and moved out into the back garden where she found a shaded bench. Now and then she glanced back at the house and caught glimpses of the few tourists who moved room to room. Alexander Braun's words came back to her: "Frida Kahlo painted her pain." Yes, Maggie thought, but it's not that simple. Frida Kahlo was proud and vain and a manipulator. And a marvelous and imaginative painter. How was Maggie to make sense of this? What could Maggie have in common with Frida Kahlo?

Well, Frida was about Maggie's age when she died. That thought depressed her. For Frida by then had a house full of paintings and the nascent acclaim of the art world. But always, even with Diego Rivera, Frida seemed to be isolated. In the photographs on the walls inside Casa Azul, and in Frida's paintings of the two of them, Frida appeared detached, alone. Well, alone was something that Maggie understood.

Maybe it was the art, the way that Frida seemed to rid herself of her pain and her scars by painting them, exaggerating them, by bravely forcing us to see and feel her pain. But how could Maggie do that? It seemed to be impossible with a camera.

"Damn you Alexander Braun," she said, and wandered back through Casa Azul. She made her way out the front door and into the splattered sunlight of Coyoacan. One night here would be enough. She would stay with her plan. Alexander Braun was an old fool, and for a time Maggie had been taken in by his know-it-all charm. But no more. She would find a hotel nearby, treat herself to a special dinner, and get a good night's rest.

Tomorrow she would drive farther south. On to Oaxaca.

CHAPTER 6

Oaxaca was larger and more congested than Maggie had imagined, and she made the mistake of driving in late in the afternoon. A half hour earlier, at four o'clock, the daily siesta time had ended, and now the shopkeepers had raised the metal storefront grates and swung open their doors, and the streets swelled with cars and trucks and buses and shoppers haphazardly crisscrossing back and forth as the mood struck them.

The street names changed inexplicably, sometimes more than once, and the Mexican men, so gracious in person, honked and fumed and shook their fists in exasperation when Maggie slowed, hoping to orient herself with a glance at the city map open on the seat beside her.

Finally she spotted *Las Golondrinas*, a small hotel she had found in a guide, four blocks or so west of the zócalo, on *calle Tinoco y Palacios*. The simple rooms, half hidden by a profusion of magenta bougainvillea, stair-stepped up the side of a hill lined with trees filled with oranges and limes and mangoes. Maggie carried her camera and followed the room clerk and his assistant—a boy she figured to be no more than twelve—who struggled with her luggage. They passed a tiny open courtyard that doubled as the ho-tel's cafe. Banana trees and what she guessed were a half-dozen papaya trees shaded the wrought-iron tables and chairs. This was the Mexico charm she had been waiting for.

The courtyard was empty except for one couple at a corner table. They looked up from their drinks and nodded as Maggie passed. Something about them—the woman's chopped-off blond hair, the man's hiking shorts and boots—told Maggie they were European, maybe German or Swedish. Maggie smiled, holding in her excitement. Finally, the promise of something exotic. The man went back to the open pages of *El Mundo*, and Maggie caught part of a headline, something she read as "BLOOD FLOWS IN OAXACA." She had been told that all the Mexican newspapers used lurid headlines, so just shook her head, happy that her blood hadn't flowed from a collision. The woman flipped through what appeared to be a language textbook.

In two trips the room clerk and his helper emptied the Blazer, and by the time they finished, the room was stacked with three soft suitcases and a slide projector. A collapsed tripod leaned against the room's only chair. An assortment of bulging plastic sacks, filled with what, Maggie could not remember, lay strewn across the bed.

The room was tiny, and she could hear the hum of a fan in an adjoining room. But the place possessed a quaint handcrafted quality that had her nodding in approval as she gazed around. Rough-cut planks for a ceiling, and the plastered walls were tinted the faint color of bleached bones; the floor sparkled with patterned blue and white tiles.

For a bonus the room was easily affordable—Maggie calculated the pesos once more to make sure she was right. Seventeen dollars and some pennies a night. Yes! This would be home, for a while at least.

CHAPTER 7

Oaxaca renewed Maggie, opened her eyes once again to possibilities. She prowled the streets with her camera, hugged it ready at her side and fingered its smoothness. Off-key sounds echoed through the narrow alleyways, bouncing off the walls of ancient buildings. Lush, overripe smells wafted from hidden cafes and storefront markets and packed city buses. Sweet and sour, rancid and perfumed.

Sometimes Maggie lifted the camera and sighted through its lens, but didn't snap the shutter. She used the lens to focus and condense or fragment the continuous whirl and mix that enveloped her. The camera functioned as her third eye. Maggie loved her Olympus, its precision, its flawless mechanics. A box with a hole, perhaps, but glorified to the heavens.

She stumbled upon a camera shop near the center of town and dumped her tote bag of exposed film on the counter. These rolls documented her trip down through San Miguel and Mexico City. She felt that these shots after San Miguel had been more ambitious, that she was learning to be more judicious.

The clerk sorted through them. "Tomorrow after five," he said.

"Tomorrow?" Maggie had expected it to take a week, at least.

The clerk pointed through the glass partition behind him. There, while they watched, a sleek machine churned out sheets of snapshots.

Mexico. You can't drink the water or get a decent pillow in a hotel, or flush toilet tissue down the john. But you can get color slides developed in one day.

Earlier, as she had wandered the several blocks from her hotel to the zócalo, Maggie had come upon a man, a businessman by his appearance, who stopped for a minute in the shade of a building. He spoke rapidly into a corner pay phone, absorbed in some high-powered business deal (or contacting his lover?). Next to him a squat woman waited for a bus. She was barefoot, her toes swollen with callouses. She wore faded traditional dress—*Zapotec*, Maggie would later learn—and carried on her back, wrapped and almost hidden in her reboso, a full-grown turkey that cocked its head at Maggie when she stared. So many layers here, as if the past four hundred years had been sandwiched together and smashed flat, and now these odd, unrelated elements mingled strangely together. Or oozed out the sides.

Now Maggie hesitated in the doorway of the camera shop, undecided where to go. Okay, Maggie, she thought. Get real. In twenty-four hours you will pick up your slides, set up your projector, and see if you've made some progress. Then decide how to go from there. This will lead you on a journey. One journey or another. It won't be the end of the world. She was too hard on herself, on her talent. She had tried, without success, to shift much of the blame for her disappointment in San Miguel to the full moon. And Maggie already had glimpsed the end of the world through her mother's slow death—not in a roll of film.

But still Maggie felt the possibility of disappointment run through her, and she fought off a wave of creeping despair.

What if these slides weren't good enough either? Or lacked imagination? She had worked hard, trying to open up some underlying thematic strength, something that she would now recognize in a grand "Aha!" moment.

But what if the slides were still ordinary? Ordinary. The worst scenario Maggie could imagine. For she had fought against the ordinary all of her life—at least the past few years—and still shrank from its lukewarm embrace.

What would she do then? If only Michelle were here. They would find something to celebrate, something that cried out for a margarita, and Michelle would laugh off Maggie's doubts.

But Michelle wasn't here. Maggie was alone. Oh, well. She took a deep breath and stepped out, slowly moving up the street. For now, taking the rest of today and tomorrow off would be good, a time for her to wander the city and not take even one photograph. Just meander here and there, poke into back streets and alleyways, and hop buses to wherever. She would play tourist until tomorrow at five, and then evaluate the slides. What would follow, she couldn't know. "Let it go, girlfriend," she heard Michelle say.

"Okay," Maggie answered. "But I need something to hold onto."

The next morning Maggie left Las Golondrinas early and strolled downhill toward the zócalo. The afternoon before, as she had planned, she played tourist, lazing over a late lunch at *La Parilla*, then luxuriating in an extended siesta that left her lethargic, content to sip guava juice in the hotel courtyard. She flipped through guide books until splashy birds fluttered in to roost and fuss in the shadowy trees above her. But now, she resolved not to let the rest of this day slip by so easily.

Buses rattled past her down the hill, trailing black spumes of exhaust. Maggie stopped and held her breath until they passed. A taxi slowed for her, but she waved the driver on. Just south of the zócalo sprawled the Benito Juárez market. Already the place reverberated with screaming chickens and squealing pigs. Butchered, bloody carcasses hung in the open air. Maggie felt dizzy; her stomach rumbled its discontent, and she fled back to the open streets.

Several blocks west she came upon the Soledad Church. Inside, the Virgin of Solitude, stunning in her black velvet robe, dominated the altar. A priest—ruddy-faced and ruddy-haired (were the Irish everywhere?)—mumbled a mixture of Latin and Spanish into a microphone. A dozen black-scarfed, forlorn-faced women hunched in the pews before him.

The drone of the priest's voice followed Maggie back outside, where she wandered under the canopy of trees that shaded a smooth stoned plaza. There Maggie discovered a half-dozen vendors had set up shop, their tiny stalls crammed with gleaming cylinders of ice cream embedded in tubs of crushed ice. The chalkboards offered a score of flavors. Maggie asked about tuna, and was tempted after she learned that the flavor came from the fruit of the prickly pear—not concocted from canned fish. She eyed the leche quemado (scalded milk—a happy accident?), but finally settled for a double dip of rose-petal ice cream.

She moved to a table, eager to taste her dish of ice cream and soak up the bustle of the Oaxacan morning. From there Maggie watched the ice cream vendor in her stall. The woman folded napkins and stacked long spoons and sorted two sizes of clear glass ice cream dishes. She wiped the counter down with a wet rag, and with a stubby end of chalk added to her day's menu of flavors. The woman seemed content, proud of the work that was hers.

Her industry and her pride somehow transferred over to Maggie, and for one rising moment she felt at ease. If this poor woman can find a satisfying life serving her homemade ice cream day after day, then Maggie had hope.

She tried to see herself, an American woman, alone in Oaxaca, savoring the sweet silkiness of rose petal ice cream. Who could have guessed this? She laughed. And so far south in Mexico. Maggie had come a long way—a thousand miles from Houston. But farther than that, in ways that miles couldn't measure. Now, as she spooned the last pink creaminess from the bottom of her dish, she could hardly believe it. "Girl," she heard Michelle say, "you have arrived."

Then, suddenly, for no reason she could know, Maggie felt herself spiral down and go flat, as quickly as she had elevated. It was as if sitting there next to the church she sensed something that was missing. Could it be Kelly? She didn't think so. He needed to make his own life. Maggie, with all of her advice and encouragement (and nagging), would be no help at all. Kelly didn't need his well-intentioned mom. Not now. He had to work things out for himself.

Maybe she missed Michelle? She was a hoot, and a dear friend, but if Michelle were here she would pull and prod and direct Maggie this way and that, keeping her distracted, always on the move. With Michelle leading the way, Maggie would spend her days and nights suspended in that nether-world between being high and hungover. It would be, "Let's go here, let's do that," and too easy for Maggie to follow along. With her pal around, Maggie could forget about her work, whatever that might turn out to be.

That left Gordon. Maybe it was Gordon that she missed, something that she refused to acknowledge out loud, something she would never admit. Not even to Michelle. No, especially not to her friend.

She sensed Michelle next to her, shaking her head with disapproval. "Hey, Michelle," Maggie whispered. "Get off my case." She nudged the air with her elbow, into her imaginary friend's ribs. "You drop your bad habits and I'll get rid of mine."

Whether good or bad, habits were hard to shake. Twenty-something-year-old habits, especially. Sometimes over those years, Gordon had been okay. At least he was someone to pal around with, a semi-warm body to sit across from in a restaurant. And oh, how Maggie hated to eat alone.

She felt her sadness rise, make its way to her throat and then her eyes. "Oh, Maggie," she murmured, and wiped the back of her hand across her nose. "You're toting a Blazer full of baggage."

The ice cream vendor came from around the stall. She took Maggie's empty dish, and for a moment stood there, giving Maggie time to speak, to tell her what was wrong. But Maggie stared off to her right where a man struggled with a cart overloaded with blocks of ice.

The woman moved back behind the stall and dipped Maggie's empty dish and spoon into a plastic bucket of water. She sloshed them up and down a couple of times, the gray, sudsless water from the bucket splashing out on the stone pavers. Then she placed them back on the counter, ready for the next customer.

Maggie napped until late afternoon, waiting for stomach cramps to hit her. Tablets of Immodil and a prescription bottle of Bactrin F sat on the bedside table. But Maggie awoke at four, surprised to feel terrific. The slump of the morning had vanished with her long nap. It had just been exhaustion, she reasoned. And why not? More than a week on the road, some days driving hundreds of miles, sleeping on straw-filled mattresses and those damn crunchy foam-cube pillows. Who wouldn't be exhausted? Who wouldn't sink a little?

By the time she showered and dressed and got back down to the street it was late, and she turned toward the center of town, where she found a table under the portal of the Restaurant Del Jardín. From there she looked out over the plaza and watched the late afternoon promenade begin. She studied a menu, glancing back and forth at a young couple cuddled on a secluded bench. Oh, what they would give for the backseat of an old Chevy, Maggie thought with a smile. A nostalgic smile.

She waved off the table-hopping hawkers, loaded down with carved and dotted animals and beaded bracelets and finely incised and decorated gourds. Later, she thought, before I leave. Too soon to even think about that.

From the bandstand in the center of the zócalo came a cacophony of sound as a military band tuned its brass, preparing for the evening's concert. How marvelous, Maggie thought, a shaded park in the middle of the city surrounded on all sides by streets with no cars, and sidewalks lined with cafes. And a free concert. What a civilized way to live. But then from up the street a crowd moved toward the zócalo. At first Maggie figured it was a parade of some sort, for the leaders held high a wide banner. But the banner turned out to be a student protest against censorship at the university.

The crowd, young men and women both, chanted and shouted, and some tried to climb on the bandstand. A waiter stood by Maggie's table and watched as uniformed men with helmets and batons rushed the bandstand and dispersed the crowd with swings of the batons and their overpowering numbers.

Maggie rose from her chair. "What's happening?" she asked the waiter. He just shook his head and wiped down a table. "Todos las dias," he said. "It's okay. Students one day, teachers the next."

Then things began to quiet down. Maggie, a little shaken, almost ordered a margarita; but quickly the musicians once more began tuning their instruments and the shoeshine men popped their rags, busy again, as if life has to go on. Maggie whispered to herself, "acceptance, acceptance." Not easy. She sighed and asked for a lemonade. The waiter nodded and quickly brought a bowl of spicy, red-skinned peanuts along with her drink. She stirred through the nuts with her finger and found tiny cloves of roasted garlic to nibble. Life does go on, until it doesn't. She had a lot to learn here in Oaxaca. Enjoy the moment, she thought.

The peanuts were fried, slippery to her fingers, but like everything she had ordered here, were scrumptious. Probably it's the lard they fry everything in, she figured. But lard might be okay for Maggie, along with mounds of fresh butter, and baskets of *pan dulces*, and tumblers of *cerveza*, and lots of grilled carne asada. Why not? Life sure doesn't come with much of a warranty. Not if you read the not-so-small print.

Maggie figured she would be alone from now on, anyway. Why drag out all of those lonely years with clean living? All at once she longed for a shot of tequila, that easy escape, but decided that tequila might accelerate the process too much.

Instead, she savored a plate of sliced fruit—bananas and mangoes and papaya smothered with silky yogurt and a sprinkling of cinnamon.

Now, with a smug feeling of purity and self-rightousness Maggie wandered north, up Alcalá, a pedestrian-only street of shops and galleries and cafes. From a sidewalk vendor she found the perfect blouse for Michelle. A girl—she couldn't have been more than ten—held it up, proudly pointing

46

out how she had embroidered ("By hand! By hand!") a village scene stitched in a curve that followed the neckline. One that featured a circle of girls holding hands while men sprawled out around them, tequila bottles in hand. Maggie couldn't say no.

In the *Galleria de las Tres Palomas* Maggie lusted for a hand-woven rug from the village of *Teotitlán del Valle*. It was wool and woven with abstract designs in all-natural colors. This is art, Maggie thought, a painting in fabric. No way it would go on a floor, it belonged stretched and hung on a wall. She fingered the price tag, and a lumpy Señora, decked out in a native skirt and Guatemalan huipil that gave her a comical costume party look, hurried over.

"A very good buy," she said. "For two months the weaver must work. Two months! All by hand. Everything by hand. He shears the wool, mixes the dyes from plants that grow in the mountains. He works at the loom for weeks and weeks. All for one rug! *Que lastima*," she said. The woman put her hand to her forehead as if she would faint. She sighed. "So much work."

Maggie was gracious, and agreed that, yes, it was a fine rug, and that it must take tremendous work. But she was only looking, for now. "I will be here in Oaxaca for a while," Maggie said. "Maybe for a long while."

"That is good," the woman said. Her eyes lit up with tiny silver sparks. She introduced herself as Señora Velez. "I am now a widow," she said, with sadness or relief, Maggie wasn't sure.

"Perhaps you would like to take an art class?" Señora Velez asked. "It begins in ten days, but there is a discount if you sign up early. The class will be for six weeks. Many classes. Three days a week. Or maybe more. Who can know? A famous painter of watercolors is here," she said proudly. "A professor from the United States. From Texas."

"No, I don't think so," Maggie said, backing away.

"The classes, they are very cheap," Señora Velez said. "For an American lady it is nothing."

"I'll think about it," Maggie said, and moved out the door, back into the late afternoon shadows of the street.

In another shop she flipped through a rack of postcards, photographs of the gilded church of Santo Domingo up the street, and the bounty of the markets, and the ruins of Monte Albán. I could do this, Maggie thought. I could take these kinds of photographs for postcards, but better. For the images were ordinary and straightforward, nothing imaginative or unique at all. She scribbled down the name and the address of the distributor in Mexico

City. Postcards are one possibility, she told herself. But even as she said it, she shook her head. Maggie knew she had to stop assessing everything in terms of dollars. Another old habit. For with the sale of the Houston house, money was not an immediate problem.

Now she must take the time to discover her own work. Maggie deserved this chance. "You need to loosen up, girlfriend," Michelle whispered.

The slides weren't ready at five o'clock, and not at six, either, when Maggie returned to the shop after a Cubana sandwich at Del Jardín. Maggie's impatience seemed to have little effect on the store manager. He shrugged, held out his hands, palms up, in a helpless way. In Mexico, Maggie knew, time has an on-again, off-again relationship to the calendar. But to the clock, too?

Before seven Maggie hurried back to Las Golondrinas, finally clutching her carton of slides. Washed-out streetlights flickered on and cast shadows across the city's sidewalks. She pushed through the hotel's weathered doors and past the front desk. Geronimo, the night clerk, looked up from the little television on the counter and nodded. Maggie caught a glimpse of a boxing match on the screen as she hurried through the tiny lobby and out the back door. She moved up the stone steps, past the deserted patio, ducking under a limb that drooped, heavy with limes. At her room she stopped to dig in her purse for the key and for a moment breathed in the sweet perfume of the night. Yes, she thought. This is the moment of truth.

Maggie filled two carousels with slides and watched as the images flashed onto the stucco wall before her. She sat barefoot, cross-legged on the bed, and clicked the slides forward. Churches and mountains and roadside capillas. One of cactus blossoms with a wad of worker bees inside—she swore she could hear the buzz—and burros and crosses and markets and colorful doors, and on and on appeared before her. But no children or beggars or stacks of red chiles. That was an improvement. She was good. Technically, most of the images were fine. She recognized the ones she had taken when the light was low or the object too distant or the viewfinder too cluttered and busy for the shot to have a focal point. Those failings didn't bother her. Better to take the shot and fail, than to let the chance of a good image never enter the camera's shutter.

After the last slide flashed by, Maggie sat on the bed in the dark. She could hear voices from the room across the way. A man and a woman. One low and reasonable, the other high-pitched and angry. Conflict and struggle were everywhere, it seemed. All over the world, in every language.

Except in her slides. That was still the problem. Her problem. "Damn!" Maggie whispered. She had captured the lovely, and even the poignant. The slides of some oddities—a goat tethered in front of a mural filled with painted goats, and some clever juxtapositions of the old and the new. An oxen pulling a plow in a field with the vapor stream from a jet above. She had an eye that captured odd moments like that, the uncommon set against the backdrop of the ordinary.

But that wasn't enough. Postcard art. Good postcard art. Pretty and clever and occasionally cute. Cute! Oh, how Maggie hated that word.

She unplugged the projector, tossed the extension cord to one side so that she could pace the room. But pacing was next to impossible. Three steps this way and three steps back. "Damn," she murmured. With every step, "Damn! Damn! Damn!"

Maggie moved out the door and down the dozen steps to the patio. The night was clear, but the city's glow hid all but the brightest of stars. A slight breeze stirred the trees. Out on the street a bus geared down to a stop, then with a groan moved on up the hill.

Alone in the dark, she forced her mind back, trying to find some beginning point, thinking that if she could understand where everything started, then she could follow the events of her life, one at a time, and understand how she arrived here, alone, in the courtyard of the Las Golondrinas hotel. If she could do that then everything, or something, would surely make sense, and she would know what to do next.

But there seemed to be no orderly pattern of events. Her mind raced through a mishmash of the ephemeral and the too real.

The photographs from her first class with Michelle, a dozen artsy black and white images of an abandoned carousel. Close-ups of the horses' eyes, some deliberately out of focus to give the horses a sense of ghostly movement. A fine first effort, Michelle had told her. The ambition of those shots created the bridge to their friendship.

Those same black and white photos in a manila folder she handed to Gordon when he came in from work. Without even a cursory glance he tossed the folder on a side table, telling Maggie he would "check them out as soon as I have a drink, as soon as the news is over." The photographs stayed there, the folder unopened on that table, for five more weeks, until Maggie put them away.

CHAPTER 8

But during that restless night, Frida and Maggie's mother, in Maggie's mostly hypnogogic dreams, with their suffering and their sorrow, their scars and their anger, woke Maggie to an answer, one that had been right before her all along. Morning couldn't arrive early enough, and at 8:00 Maggie hurried to the center of town. At the *sitio* next to the zócalo she caught a taxi for the fifteen-minute ride north to the regional medical center. There she explained to the receptionist as best she could that a friend of Dr. Reyes had referred her there. An old friend in Texas, a Dr. Ramsey.

The woman nodded and said she understood. Dr. Reyes had not come in yet, but he would be with her before long. She studied her watch. "Before ten o'clock," she said. "I am certain."

Maggie waited in a room of colicky babies and dark, pregnant women. Posters on the wall cautioned vigilance against cholera and diarrhea, hepatitis and malaria. "Lord help us all," Maggie whispered, and moved next to a half-open window where she could breathe the fresh air.

It was almost 11:00 when the receptionist motioned to Maggie and led her back through a maze of chalky-green hallways to a small and simple office. Dr. Reyes greeted her warmly. He was a tall man, by Oaxacan standards, with melancholy eyes.

He spoke faultless English, and Maggie relaxed, relieved that he spoke so easily in her language. For every conversation in Spanish took immense concentration and effort. Dr. Reyes spoke fondly of his old friend Dr. Ramsey with warmth and some vague longing in his voice.

"Can I help you in some way?" he finally asked.

Maggie took a deep breath. "Yes," she said. "Perhaps you can." And Maggie laid out her plan, what she now was determined to photograph and why. She explained that she needed his help—someone's help—in order to make it work.

Dr. Reyes listened intently, and when Maggie had finished he waited a moment. He nodded. Finally with a dramatic gesture he drew a fountain pen from his pocket as if it were a sword, and attacked a single sheet of his letterhead. He wrote silently for several minutes, and then on a separate sheet scribbled the names of three outlying villages, along with how to contact their mayors. He rose and handed both sheets to Maggie. He gave a slight bow. "This is a unique idea," he said. "It will be a book?" he asked.

"Yes," Maggie said without thinking. "Yes, it will be a book." Her heart raced with the small deception, but more with the realization that someone else might understand her vision and validate it.

"It could be good work," he said. "Not only as photographs, your art, but perhaps to help these poor people. Certainly it will do no harm."

Maggie trembled as she left the clinic and danced away to the street.

"A book," she said to a puzzled taxi driver who was leaning against his cab. "I have an idea, a unique idea, for a book."

The next three weeks whirled by for Maggie, a spinning dream of rough roads and remote villages. Maggie spent hours waiting in the small municipal offices and on benches in simple plazas. She waited while suspicious men passed Dr. Reyes's letter around, most often speaking that strange Zapotec language that excluded Maggie completely. "You must come back next week," they said. Or, "It is necessary to talk with the shaman when he returns from the mountain."

Finally, she gained permission from the elders of one village and spent a Saturday there with her camera. But that day seemed no more than a shard she had uncovered at the edge of a dig. She needed more, but Maggie felt the resistance, the distrust of the village's elders. And now all sorts of ideas raced through her head. If only she had done this, said that. If only she could work that first village one more time, or better, move on to the next one. But for now she waited. She walked Oaxaca and she waited.

CHAPTER 9

Whether he first heard the trumpets or the fireworks or the dogs Connor could not remember. But now fully awake, he shifted diagonally across the double bed so that his toes no longer touched the footboard, and he listened. In the dark the clock across the room glowed 9:28. Connor would have guessed later, even 1:00 or 2:00 in the morning, but Mexico had disoriented him from the beginning. Or maybe mezcal had messed up his sense of time.

For a few more minutes he sat on the edge of the bed in his jockey shorts and waited. He ran his hands through his black, combed-straight-back hair and pulled on the tangled ends—still too short for even a trace of a pony tail. But that would happen. Now that he was in Oaxaca and no longer at that gospel-saturated university in Abilene, he could do, or be, whatever he damned well wanted.

The fireworks boomed again in the night and quick-flashed through his small room, illuminating cracked plaster walls and the low ceiling that held a length of galvanized water pipe and a bare bulb hanging from a twist of wire. He moved out the door and onto the still-warm stones of the balcony and settled into a black wrought-iron chair. From there, on the second floor of this ancient building, he could catch a glimpse up the hill of the dimly lit street, the scattering of lights casting their dingy yellow glow. Connor glanced across the courtyard to the small room where Rafael stayed most nights, but it was dark.

The distant sound of trumpets still, probably, several blocks away, faded in and out with the wind, but now he could pick up the deep whine of saxophones and the background beat of a bass drum.

The dogs started up once more, their howling and barking either in protest or warning, or, who could know, perhaps trying to join the cacophony of the approaching band in their unique mongrel ways. For these were Mexican dogs, and Connor had been in Oaxaca long enough to know them without seeing, the dogs yellow and skinny-ribbed, roaming up and down the ragged alleys, padding lazily through the rivulets of gray water that trickled down forever across the stone streets. The dogs' pee, raised leg high, stained the stone walls of the buildings. Guard dogs paced the roofs of the city, growling, barking down at the streets below, their paws positioned between shards of broken glass at the roofs' edges. The dogs howled and bred and fought, especially at night, while Connor, the sleepless gringo, pulled a crunchy foam pillow over his ears.

Sounds filled the city, and from his three weeks here Connor knew them all. Two distinct whistles, the one-note flute sound of the postman as he made his rounds with the mail, and the higher-pitched whistle of the knife sharpener as he pushed his bicycle with its grinder wheel contraption through the streets; there was the clear tingle of a metal rod inside the triangle that hung from the top of the ice cream vendor's cart; the frantic clang of the garbage truck's bell and the slam of doors as maids and wives ran with bulging plastic bags to the street; the hollow bong of a wooden club against an empty gas cylinder as a propane truck groaned slowly around the block and a big-voiced boy riding in back shouted GAS! GAS! every half-block; the pop of a rag as the shoeshine man waited below to see if Connor would move to the front of the balcony and toss down his boots; the water truck, its giant bottles gleaming in the morning sun, a man riding the rear bumper, hanging on with one hand, his head thrown back, singing out his aria of "agua, super agua," over and over again; then the doorbell buzzing downstairs—boys, rags in hand, hoping to wash a car; Señoras delivering deep baskets of tortillas. And always Rafael, bent over in the courtyard, snapping his grass clippers as he eased across the lawn that surrounded the koi pond below. Most days ended with a military band's flag-lowering wave of music from the zócalo; then always traffic, bad mufflers blatting and boom boxes booming and car horns honking and then, finally, just at dark, church bells ringing their summons. And almost always, inevitably, the fireworks, for no reason that Connor understood at all.

But earlier that evening, sitting inside at the Del Jardín bar on the zócalo, Connor had heard other, more disturbing sounds—yells and chants, and, then, from somewhere to the southeast, how far away Connor could not tell, something—more fireworks? Or gunfire? Teachers from all over the state of Oaxaca had gathered there, still striking, he knew, marching with their placards. This had been going on for more than his three weeks. Every night the same. Shouting, chanting, marching around the zócalo, and then moving out of the town's center, toward the university. What good had that ever done here in this poor-ass state of Oaxaca?

Rafael kept him informed, seemed to be involved in some way, Connor could tell, but the last thing he wanted was conflict and problems—Connor hoped he had left those behind. But he worried that the turmoil would keep the tourists away, especially the tourists who had signed up for his watercolor classes at Señora Velez's gallery.

But now from the balcony outside his room, the sounds of the band jolted him back. He pushed up from his chair and moved to the edge of the balcony where he could see the street. The band must be moving slowly toward him, up Alcalá.

What was today, anyway? So many celebrations. Some band, it seemed, was always marching and playing. There were weddings and funerals and holidays of the state and special days of the church. The music sounded all the same to Connor. The musicians marched up and down the streets playing their same three songs over and over again. Only the tempo changed; the tempo now was fervent and upbeat. Maybe even angry.

By now Connor was ten days into the middle of a fall watercolor workshop, a visiting artist teaching three mornings a week, and the rest of the time spent (supposedly) working on his own impressions of Oaxaca and the surrounding villages. A sweet deal, considering his diminished options. All of this would culminate, if things went as planned, in a show that would open the first of November, a few weeks from now.

But Connor had run into a lot of uncertainties about exactly when the show would take place, and if it would be his one-man show, as Señora Velez had promised; the only certainty was that it would be held in the street-level gallery below. But he could live with a few unknowns since Señora Velez raised the pesos for the workshop through some quasi-government arts program in addition to the students' fees, and Connor felt himself lucky to be on the receiving end.

The money involved was minimal, just a lump sum for transportation from Texas to Oaxaca, and a small weekly stipend, plus this room above the art gallery, the Galeria de las Tres Palomas. When this opportunity came out of nowhere Connor raked together some small savings he had and headed south, economizing by taking a bus down from Laredo. The buses, he had heard, were now genuinely first class, and they may have been—somewhere else—but he had caught the best bus that Tres Estrellas offered and rode three days, sipping tequila Conmemorativo when he couldn't sleep. The floor of the bus seeped a precarious and unidentifiable slickness, and Connor's very soul filled with the blackness of spent diesel fuel and the stench from an overripe toilet. Connor hunkered down in the back while the bus rocked and swayed and roared deep into Mexico.

Now Connor had recovered from the trip and was adjusting. He taught and painted in an airy downstairs room that had been renovated at the rear of the gallery courtyard. Windows opened onto a lawn with fountains and stone paths and the tiled fishpond. There a couple of caged macaws complained each morning while Rafael chopped their fruit and refilled their tin cups of water. From above, Connor often watched Rafael, admired his classic looks, his intelligent face, the way the morning sun gleamed off the darkness of his hair. Although Connor figured Rafael to be young, no more than twenty-five and from a working-class family, he always wore a thin gold chain that swayed across his chest as he worked. He moved with sureness, with grace, whether sweeping the courtyard paths, trimming the towering bougainvilleas that threatened to overrun the place, or helping Señora Velez hang a new painting.

Rafael's home lay somewhere outside of Oaxaca, near the small town of Coyotepec. But during the week he stayed in a tiny upstairs room, formerly servants' quarters, across the courtyard from Connor. Most mornings, if Connor rose early enough, he wandered around the balcony that completely circled the courtyard, taking his time, sipping his cup of black coffee. When

Rafael's door opened, Connor would stop by for a few minutes while the young man heated water for his chocolate con agua.

Rafael's room was spare, a cot on one side, just a bare thin mattress with a wool blanket kicked back at one end, and a wall-hung sink with a single faucet. A toilet hid behind a faded muslin curtain. A small pine table held a hot plate, some odd glasses and plates, a tin spoon, and a fork. A couple of water pipes stretched across the ceiling of the room; a single clear light bulb hung from a pigtail of twisted wires and gave off a sickly yellow light. A butcher knife, its handle wrapped in frayed duct tape, lay next to an ever-present papaya half. Connor always marveled at the salmon-colored flesh of the fruit, the black seeds that glistened like tiny marbles.

Connor would mostly ask questions, practicing his Spanish, and Rafael would answer in English, for it turned out he was enrolled part time at the Benito Juárez Autonomous University of Oaxaca, a mile or so southeast of the zócalo. Rafael called this exchange in two languages *intercambio*, referring to Connor as *profesor*, while Connor called Rafael his *maestro*. At the university Rafael had sat in on political science courses for the past year, hoping to become a lawyer someday. And if Connor didn't interrupt him, Rafael would complain, and then begin to shout, about the inequities, the plight of the poor, which included his own family, who lived fifteen kilometers south of Oaxaca. Those he knew about first hand. So when he could, Connor would change the subject of Rafael's rants by asking about his parents, his family.

"Yes, I have a wife, and a son, too. Carlos is nearly four years old," Rafael would take a deep breath, trying to unwind. He stirred his chocolate while he spoke. "And we live in the house of my parents. It is only four rooms, but it is enough, for I am here most of my days." He swept his arm around the room, not in a gesture of anger or resentment, but one simply of fact. "I go home on Sundays, if Señora Velez does not need me for the gallery."

"Is that a problem?" Connor asked. "Living away from your family most of the week?"

Rafael shrugged. "It is better than my brothers, who make pottery, over and over again, or my father, plowing his field of corn on the side of a hill behind two slow oxen.

"My mother and her sister, they also make barro negro pottery, the famous black pottery of Coyotepec." He nodded. "They are very good, real artists, like many of my family in that place. But the man they work for pays them too little."

"So it is good to be here." Then he added, "For now, while I am in the university." He gestured toward the gallery. "Here I meet interesting people, some from America, some from Europe, even Paris. From everywhere. All of them are very rich. And I will finish the university in two more years and maybe I will be rich, too." Rafael pulled on his windbreaker. "See you later," he said. "Have a nice day."

"Very good, Rafael," Connor said with a laugh. "Just like an Americano." He watched as Rafael hurried across the balcony to the limestone stairs that curved down to the courtyard, taking the steps two at a time, and in a moment disappeared out the front gate.

Connor had known young men like Rafael before. They lived everywhere. And whether in Texas or California or Mexico they all needed to be around those with power, with money, as if mixing with those wealthy people gave them the chance to become more than they were, even if only in their dreams. We all need our dreams, Connor thought, although his own dreams, of late, had been pretty grim.

But Connor found an escape from himself in observing Rafael, wondering how the young Mexican lived. Surely this centuries-old building, somewhat run down now, but still with an opulent air, must be foreign to him, to the simple way he lives with his wife's parents. In what? Some shack in Coyotepec? And Rafael's wife? To be with him she must be young, too, and attractive. But would she resent that her husband, dressed in clean jeans and a white shirt, caught the bus into the city, attended classes at the university, mingled with artists of all kinds at the gallery, while she stayed behind? Connor didn't think so, but he couldn't know, couldn't even quite imagine. He did know what Jeanie, his soon-to-be ex-wife, now living in Houston, would think about it.

Thoughts like this rambled through Connor's mind while he painted, and also when he wandered through the studio, commenting gently, not quite honestly, on his students' attempts at watercolor, attempts that always seemed to fall short of competent. For Connor's students disappointingly had turned out to be ordinary, mostly gray-haired gringas down in Oaxaca for a little subdued adventure. They were joined by a few young and earnest locals, who seemed to have given up and dropped out of the rigid approach to art at the university.

But his students for the most part were easy, not demanding at all, and seemed to respect Connor and his talent. And unlike art students back at the university in Texas, these students listened, followed Connor's directions, and reacted gracefully to the criticisms and suggestions from their wise professor. A bonus of teaching this class, he knew, but hated to acknowledge, was the absence of the temptations that had brought on so much turmoil in the past year. No lovely young and eager female graduate students. Not even one in this group, he sadly conceded.

Those first weeks of being alone in Oaxaca had freed him, and now he felt this new life assert itself, as he drifted away from the sour times in Texas. He slipped easily among the crowds that strolled the zócalo at dark. He sipped lemonadas or cold Bohemias laced with the tartness of tiny Mexican limes, sampling in three days seven distinct blends and colors of mole, puzzling through heaping baskets of pan dulces for breakfast.

The varieties of mezcal seemed endless—flavored anise or orange or pineapple, with and without the worm. At a tiny stall at the fringes of the Ocotlán Friday market, a curandera steeped her homemade mezcal with a mix of bitter herbs and claimed it would cure Connor's illness. When he objected, told her he was well, she took his hand in hers and shook her head. "No, you need this. I see a tragedy in your future. You must drink a little mezcal every day, to make your life bearable." Connor gave a nervous laugh. He didn't believe in all that herbal, mystical nonsense. The last thing he needed was this old woman's *bruja* hocus-pocus. But Connor eased back into the crowded market toting a liter of her magical mezcal.

By now the little Oaxacan band had passed the gallery and moved on up Alcalá. The night fell almost quiet once more, except for the continuing chorus of turned-on dogs and the whine of a distant bus. Connor felt hopelessly awake. He wished that he still smoked. That's what the tragic hero would do if this were a movie. He could envision it—the off-key band rag-tagging its way past his window, the flash and spew of Roman candles illuminating the solitary figure of a lonely man on the balcony, smoking.

But Connor was no hero, and his life no more tragic than those of thousands or millions of other men. And the minor tragedies—his abandonment by Jeanie, his wife of twenty-four years, the loss of a university position that he had held almost half that long, his virtual alienation from Claire, his only child, now in Alaska, separated perhaps for who could know how long— these were events that Connor had allowed to happen. Early on Jeanie apparently had been attracted to Connor's charm, his rueful grin, an attraction that lasted until she discovered that those traits reflected a boyish helplessness and unreliability that proved not so charming to live with.

And here, after the first three weeks of excitement and high expectations, the everyday reality of being in Mexico had hit him hard. The filling his days with not-quite-enough pesos, of speaking and thinking in a strange language, of being more alone than he had ever been. And worse, not knowing where he would go, what he would find to do when he ran out the string of these classes at the gallery, when he would peer into the void of not having a university position to fall back on.

Oh, well. Connor shook his head at the onset of melancholia. You're homesick, old buddy, he thought. But with no home. And Connor knew it was more than homesickness. He had been reckless and careless and insensitive. The consequences he had justly earned. Maybe he could find some way to redeem himself. But not tonight.

Back in his room, in the dark, he pulled on his jeans and a knit shirt, and slipped on his shoes. He splashed his face with a palm of water he sloshed from a plastic bottle, and ran a comb through his thinning hair. He ducked as he made his way back out the door, for Connor found the doorways and beds and bus seats too cramped for his lankiness.

Out on the street he hurried to catch up with the band, following by ear the path the band had taken. Smoke from spent fireworks drifted in soft swirls around the dim street lights, and when Connor turned left off Alcalá and reached the next corner he picked up, now louder, the echo of tinny sounds ahead that ricocheted off the stone walls. The drift of fireworks smoke dissipated across the shadowed hills in the distance, and the music faded in and out with the wind. In the lulls he picked up the distant pulsing of sirens to the southeast.

Connor stopped at an open doorway where a woman nursed her *reboso-*hidden baby. "The celebration," he asked in his best Spanish, pointing ahead. "What is it?" The woman shook her head and retreated into the dark room. The fragrance of a wood fire and the pungent essence of a bubbling stew swirled around Connor's head. In a few moments a man appeared. The white of his undershirt glowed blue in the yellow half-light. He didn't speak but gave his head a quick upward tilt in a defensive, what-do-you-want sort of way.

"Oh, the celebration, the parade," he replied when Connor asked again.

"For the people of Oaxaca it is a holy day." He looked around for his wife, but she had disappeared into the interior of the darkened house. "Perhaps it is the day of Nuestra Señora del Rosario."

His wife, from somewhere in the darkness, corrected him. "No," she said. "That is another day in this month, much later." The man looked annoyed, and Connor nodded his thanks and hurried on, past a small *tienda* where a smoking grill out front on the sidewalk held a charred mound of carnitas, and then past the ranchero music and flashing lights beyond the swinging doors of a corner bar. Back in the states Connor wouldn't have given a *frijole* for a religious holiday, but this felt different.

He moved quickly to catch the slow-moving procession. Their route had now turned north and then west again, up a narrow dirt street. Connor eased his pace when he was almost upon them, staying back thirty paces or so.

Despite the late hour people crowded the doorways and sidewalk along the street. Older women watched silently, heads nodding in approval while men sipped cervezas and small children and dogs chased after a ball rolling down a ditch. A girl stopped and pointed at Connor, drawn to his height, his pale skin. Her mother gently slapped the girl's tiny finger and whispered softly. Then they melted back into the shadow of their house.

The parade slowed, then turned from the street through a sagging wooden gate and into a fenced courtyard. The musicians seemed to exhale all at once, and the music stopped. Connor eased closer and watched from across the street, stopping self-consciously next to a light pole, leaning his shoulder easily against its smoothness as if he were resting there for only a moment and would be moving on at any time.

Past the open wooden gate, a house stretched long and low inside the courtyard. A tin-roofed porch ran the entire length of the house, and a half-dozen rickety cedar poles supported the roof. The porch overhang sheltered a series of long wooden tables and rough benches. Pink balloons hung like sausages from the rafters, and the far end of the porch glowed from the blaze of candles.

Connor moved away from the light pole and eased across the street next to the gate. In the back of the courtyard he spotted two burros working at a pile of straw, tossing their heads as they ate, while black and white chickens, jarred from their roosts by all of the commotion, fussed around the burros' legs, leaving a flurry of feathers and dust.

The men gathered together in the yard under a tree and passed back and forth what appeared to be a canning jar of mezcal. The band members drank first, each one filling a shot glass, then, with the solemnity of communion and a silent nod of thanks, quickly tossed it back.

The women had taken over the porch, moving gracefully in long, dark skirts. Their braided hair glistened in the candlelight. One of the women seated a doll-sized santo on a gold-painted throne on a table at the end of the porch. The santo's velvet robe shone like fresh blood; a giant silver heart hung around his neck and a beaded crown sat askew on the santo's head.

The women laughed and talked as they worked, their voices not the lilt, the rapid fall and rise of Mexican Spanish, but the harsh clatter of Zapotecs. They moved back and forth through the doorway of the house, carrying out vases and quart jars of lilies, first for the santo's throne, and then for each of the tables.

As if from nowhere a man appeared out of the shadow of the open gate, jolting Connor back to attention. He was a young man and slight of build. He wore white pants and a loose white shirt that fell off his narrow shoulders.

The man evidently had spotted Connor following the band, and then as he watched from the gate. Now he motioned for Connor to come, and Conner moved forward toward him a step or two. He started to explain that he was just passing by, that he had stopped there only a moment to rest, that he was on his way to his room in town when he saw the lights. But the words didn't come out quite right, and the young man once more, this time impatiently, gestured in that curious palm-down Mexican way for Connor to come.

"I have the permission of my grandfather," the man said. "You must join our celebration." He introduced himself as Leonardo and told Connor that this was his grandfather's home and led him through the gate.

Connor followed, ducking slightly as he entered. Leonardo located the jar of mezcal—for the entire evening it appeared to stay full, an authentic miracle to Connor. All of the men stopped and watched while Leonardo poured a small black clay cup full and held it out to the gringo. Thoughts of the worm and then worse, the possibility of home-brew blindness, flashed through Connor's mind, and he hesitated for a moment. Then he raised the cup first to Leonardo and then, just as a precaution, raised it upward toward the blackness of the Mexican night, a vague and futile gesture to whomever up there it might concern. With a quick tilt of his head he tossed the mezcal down.

Connor shuddered involuntarily while the onlooking men murmured their approval. "It is very strong," Leonardo whispered, "but good for a man. With the women, you know."

A numbness began to creep through Connor's body, and he figured that after more than one shot of this a man wouldn't be able even to find a woman, unless she happened to be crawling around on all fours, too.

But now the band started up once again and Connor turned back to the porch to watch as a tall, slender woman took the santo from his throne. "Claudia. My sister," Leonardo said proudly. "She lives in Coyotepec, but she came to our grandfather's house for this special night."

Connor watched as Claudia held the santo at arms' length and began to move in a slow circle dance. Something about the young woman fascinated him. Not only was she lovely, with skin that glowed in the half-light, but there was more, something intangible, a sureness about her that Connor sensed, an optimism, a freedom, that the older Mexican women seemed to lack.

Claudia quickly glanced at Connor as he watched her, but never, not for even a moment, lost her composure. She wore jeans and a faded Hard Rock Cafe T-shirt, and she appeared at ease in her family's home. While she danced, the other women began to clap in rhythm. Slowly the band re-grouped and worked into a steady tempo, slow at first, then gathering speed.

Claudia circled faster, her face radiant, her eyes fixed on the santo, until she came near the end of the porch once more where she stopped, and with a little bow and a kiss to the santo's cheek, replaced the doll on its throne.

Then another, older woman stepped forward and danced, but with a slight limp, the same circle dance. Then another and another, slender girls with downcast eyes, and stooped women defiant of their ages; they all danced with the radiance of Leonardo's sister, all with miraculous grace.

Then the women motioned for Leonardo and Connor to come, and they led them to where the santo now sat back on his throne. Connor glanced around. Everything—the music, the drinking—had stopped for a moment. Everyone watched. The women murmured. Leonardo leaned close to Connor. "They want you to kiss the santo," he whispered.

Claudia moved close to Connor—she seemed to be the one who did not mind stepping forward. She watched him for a moment, as if he were a strange creature dropped into her presence, and in that moment Connor felt drawn by the darkness of her eyes. A tiny scar cut across one corner of her mouth, the scar turned up just a little, giving Claudia what appeared to be the hint of a permanent smile. She crossed herself quickly, her right hand moving smoothly across her body. Then she stepped back and gestured to Connor to do the same.

"Teach me how," Connor said, feeling a little unsteady, a little unsure about this request. Claudia smiled and crossed herself once more, this time more slowly. And Connor crossed himself, uncertainly at first, then again and again until it felt almost natural.

Claudia's mother moved right next to the santo and kissed the doll gently on the lips. She gestured to Connor. He grimaced and shook his head; this has all gone far enough, he thought. But she took Connor's hand and pulled him forward. The women gathered round to watch. They twittered and giggled and covered their mouths with their hands. Connor could smell the sweetness of the lilies, the pungency of incense. He bent low and gave the santo a peck on the cheek.

When he straightened up, the women beamed and clapped, the band started up once more, and for Connor everything suddenly began to flow—the fluid light against the black sky, the swaying swirling colors, the asthmatic bray of the burros and the harmonic dissonance and energy of the band. And Connor felt strangely at peace with himself.

Later, everyone gathered up and down the long tables. Connor sipped warm chocolate water from a black clay bowl. The mezcal came around once more. Leonardo slid in beside him; his grandfather sat across from them. The old man smiled as he talked, his teeth worn down from years of eating tortillas made from corn ground on *metates*. He spoke to Connor, his voice hardly more than a murmur, while Leonardo quietly translated his mix of Zapotec and Spanish into English. The old man counted his family at sixty-eight—children, grandchildren, great-grandchildren, their spouses and cousins. "Many are here," he said with pride as he waved his arm around while women filled platters, all barro negro, with tamales wrapped in banana leaves. "Tomorrow," he said, "the men will cut cedar and haul it down from the mountains, and some will hoe the fields and gather beans. But tonight . . . " He stopped and with both hands raised his bowl of chocolate to Connor before he drank. Connor returned the gesture, tried to guess what this man must feel with most of his family here, knowing where he fits into this world, and having the genuine respect of at least this small group of people. Something that Connor knew he would never find for himself.

Leonardo leaned close. "How long have you been in Oaxaca?" he asked, his manner earnest. And without waiting for an answer, suddenly his questions became more pointed. "Where do you live?" Connor answered and Leonardo nodded, as if this confirmed something he already knew.

He asked what Connor did, and when Connor told him he taught art, Leonardo showed no surprise at all. He quickly asked about the women in the class that Connor taught. As Leonardo became more intense, Connor began to feel uneasy, not knowing what to make of it all. But he remained gracious even as Leonardo's voice rose. "And the woman, the pretty gringa woman who is a painter. Do you know her? What is she doing here?"

Connor had no idea what he meant. A pretty artist? He damned sure would have noticed her. But before Connor could begin to answer, Leonardo suddenly rose and a stunned Connor turned to watch him quickly move toward the street.

There, Leonardo joined Claudia just outside the gate where she was leaning forward and waving her arms as she talked to some other man, her husband or boyfriend, Connor guessed. He couldn't make out her words, but could see from her rapid gestures that this was no ordinary conversation. Leonardo stood next to them, his arms folded. The other man faced the street, his back turned to the gathering inside the courtyard. He swayed gently as he listened, as if he could hear some strange music that no one else heard. Or, perhaps he swayed to the sweet music of mezcal.

Then Connor heard a shout and the stranger swung around quickly and drew his fist back to threaten Leonardo. And Connor was stunned to see that the other man was no stranger, but Rafael, the Rafael that Connor knew from Señora Velez's gallery. Oh, Connor thought, Claudia is Rafael's wife. Yes, Leonardo had said that his sister lived in Coyotepec.

Then suddenly Rafael turned and with another shout hurried off into the night, and Claudia stepped back, crying. Leonardo took a few steps beyond the gate and shouted angrily into the dark. From all appearances Rafael had stepped over some boundary that only he and Claudia and Leonardo knew. A serious violation, obviously, and not something Connor wanted to be a part of, so he rose and nodded a silent thanks and moved off the porch toward the tree. There, he leaned against the rough bark as the band started up once more.

As he stood there, Connor began to put the pieces together: There was Leonardo's anger at some pretty woman, an artist who must have caught

Rafael's eye, and now Leonardo was defending his sister's honor. It seemed strange, though, for Connor had always thought that mistresses were accepted as a matter of course in Mexico. He had heard stories and seen movies, but this wasn't the same. In movies it was always the upper classes, the man rich and distinguished and the wife turning her head, pretending not to know. But this wasn't the same. These folks here—Leonardo's family—lived at the edge of poverty in machete land, where betrayal and infidelity might have more serious repercussions.

A woman of indeterminate age came toward him with a platter of tortillas, hot from the comal that rested on a flickering bed of coals next to the porch. Connor took one, thick and crisp, and glanced around, suddenly aware of the strangeness that surrounded him. For much of his life he had dreamed of exotic nights in a strange land. Perhaps those dreams were of Oaxaca all along. But what appeared exotic could be more layered and complex, and even more threatening than Connor could have dreamed.

CHAPTER 10

The next morning, from the balcony above the gallery, Connor watched Oaxaca come alive. A lone street sweeper scratched his broom of bundled twigs across the cobblestone. Connor followed his movements, admired his economy of motion as he worked his way from gutter to gutter, past shops and houses, and on down the street. Beyond him, a few blocks farther south, Connor spotted the morning bustle of newspaper vendors and shoeshine men rolling their mobile stands into place around the zócalo.

In the center of the courtyard below him Rafael began to clean the fish-pond. The day, once again, had broken bright and clear. And once again Connor felt like hell. More coffee, he thought, and stepped back toward his room.

By the time Connor made his way out to the balcony with his second cup of coffee, Rafael had drained the pool by hand, emptying the last few pails of murky green water in a clump of banana trees. Connor watched Rafael carefully, alert for signs of a hangover, but the young man worked as if nothing out of the ordinary had happened the night before.

For a moment Connor questioned his memory, or at least his eyesight. But no, he remembered it clearly enough—the band, the procession up the hill, then onto a side street of packed dirt, the celebration, the tamales and mezcal, the dancing. He closed his eyes, pressed his palm to his temple, and gave it a soft massage. He still could see Rafael next to Claudia and Leonardo out by the gate. He shook his head and once again watched Rafael for several minutes. Yes. It was Rafael he had seen. Without a doubt.

Connor checked his watch. His students would have begun to trickle in below and he knew that soon they—not so patiently—would be waiting. After the first three or four lessons, Connor had changed his mind about one of the women, a Maggie something, from Houston. She carried herself in a way that Connor liked, and approached her painting more boldly than the other students, who remained mostly tentative, timid. Maggie attacked the painting with broad, assertive brush strokes. And she seemed younger than Connor had guessed at first. Probably in her early forties.

Connor headed down the stairs to the courtyard and made a point of stopping by the fishpond. He greeted Rafael with his usual "Buenos dias." Rafael straightened up and nodded Connor's way. "A good day to work," he said with a grin and Connor figured he really meant it.

"We do what we have to do," Connor said.

Rafael looked around, then straight back a Connor. "Yes, we do what must be done. More than just work, sometimes."

This young fellow has plenty of good gray cells, Connor thought, not quite sure what Rafael meant. Connor pointed to the art studio. "My work," he said, and turned to leave.

"Have a good day," Rafael said, and Connor laughed.

"*Correcto*?" Rafael asked.

"*Perfecto*," Connor said. "You speak good American this morning."

"Thank you very much, profesor." Rafael grinned and reached down for a water hose. He ran a stream of fresh water into the pool while a half dozen carp-sized koi splashed about in a tub on the lawn.

Connor pointed toward the tub. "For lunch?" Connor asked. "For *comida*?"

Rafael grinned. "Why not? All they do is swim and eat and shit. They are worthless." Rafael lowered his voice. "However Señora Velez likes the fish. She wants them to have a clean pond, so I like the fish, too."

Connor tapped the side of his head with a finger. "Smart hombre," he said.

"It is the only way to be." Rafael nodded. "The only way to be and still eat."

"*Absolumente*, my friend." Connor said.

"May I ask of you a favor, Profesor? Or maybe it is too much."

"Why certainly," Connor said, with not a clue what the young man might need. Then it came to him. Yeah, probably a loan. Maybe this is why Rafael is so charming, so friendly.

"I would like a lesson," Rafael said. "A lesson in art, maybe drawing, or maybe with watercolors. Señora Velez, she must not know, however. You understand? And I could pay, at least a little. Or maybe you are too busy? For me?"

So that's Rafael's real reason to be working here at the gallery. A would-be, wanna-be artist. Well, why not? Connor thought. Clay artists were all over Coyotepec, That's what he grew up with. "So you want to be an artist," Connor said. "Well, there are worse things to do, and with hard work it is possible. Sure. I'll give you some lessons. If you have time with the classes out at the university, and your work here."

"No problem for now," Rafael said with a frown. "The university is shut down, Another protest. You know, the government, their police, took over the university radio station; they cut the subsidies for gasoline and bus fares, for tortillas and milk. It is bad for my family. For us all. Maybe no classes out there for weeks. Who can know?"

Connor shook his head. "That is bad. From Del Jardín, on the zócalo, the other night I heard sirens from that area, and maybe gunfire. Is it dangerous?"

"It is not good," Rafael said. Then he grinned. "But it gives me time for art lessons."

"Okay. It's a deal. How about two mornings a week. Early, before Señora Velez comes in. Let's meet in your room at, say, 7:30. I'll bring what you need."

"Yes, that is good." But Rafael looked worried. "I will pay you, however. It is only fair."

"How about you give me Spanish lessons? I sure could use some help with my Spanish. I'll tell you what. We'll trade. We'll both be profesores. Okay?"

"It is perfect," Rafael said. "But I am not a profesor. I know who I am."

Now Connor glanced at his watch. He was ten minutes late. "I'd better go. But, tomorrow, in the morning we will begin."

A nice young fellow, Connor thought as he hurried to the back of the courtyard. And what a surprise. Rafael, the artist.

The scene from last night, Leonardo's anger and Claudia's tears, seemed incongruous this morning, but wouldn't completely go away. Maybe Connor would have a man-to-man talk with Rafael sometime, make sure he knows what he is doing. Running around on your wife is trouble in any language. Even for an artist. Or maybe especially for an artist. Connor knew.

In the high-ceilinged studio his students were waiting, "Sorry, sorry," he said as he moved into the room, knowing that he was putting on his professor act, hiding behind his professorial voice. You do what you have to do to get by, he thought. "There was something in the air last evening," he said, "that seemed to get to me. Music, perhaps? Or maybe what was in that bottle. Oh, yes. Mezcal. Or perhaps only a gust of human frailty in that air. Regardless, the combination seems to have slowed me down this morning. But it will never happen again," he said with a wink. "I can assure you."

A couple of the women twittered and one of the other students, Eduardo, the only potential troublemaker in the class, muttered, "Yeah, sure."

The two twittering women were past middle-age, from Phoenix. That, and their names, Rena and Shirley, were all that Connor knew. He figured that they might be sisters, for they both carried around some excess pounds which they mostly covered up with those billowing, embroidered Mexican dresses.

"Seriously, sorry to be late," Connor said. "And truthfully, I stumbled into a remarkable experience last night. More on that later. But for now, let's get to work."

Today they would paint a still life of fruit—papayas, half of a small melon with rows of shiny black seeds, a small bunch of bananas, three mangos, and a pineapple—a generous and colorful pyramid that Connor had arranged on a table the afternoon before. The sun streaming through the courtyard threw a nice mix of light and shadow across the shapes and textures of the fruit, and Connor figured that this would be an interesting challenge for the group.

Surprisingly, he felt energized to be back in the studio and teaching. For he was good as a teacher and as a painter. Not great, not a genius, but accomplished, and long ago Connor had settled for that, stopped pushing the limits, stopped painting with one eye on the constantly changing art scene. And stopped fighting a battle he knew was not winnable. Here, moving around this studio of industrious students, Connor rose to a level of contentment that escaped him in most every other part of his life.

Because of time constraints, Connor, on the first day, had demonstrated how he wanted them to handle watercolors, painting wet on wet, applying pigment to the still-wet paper, and how to drop in color. Not the easiest method, but one he used for beginners working within a two-hour class time.

He turned away and moved to the back of the room where Maggie, the woman he had mostly overlooked the first couple of classes, seemed lost in concentration. She wasn't as sure with the brush as he had earlier thought, or maybe she became rattled with Connor watching over her shoulder. From behind he caught himself staring at the back of her neck, the way the fringes of her short, tapered hair moved across her skin as she turned her head side to side. For a moment he had an almost irresistible urge to brush the skin of her neck with his fingers.

But he caught himself and moved next to her, settling onto a high stool. He reminded Maggie of his comments the day before, the way to use the white of the paper for highlights, for the illusion of depth and perspective. "Here," he said, "Let me show you what I mean."

Maggie hesitated a moment, then handed him the brush. Connor felt her eyes on him, as if she were trying to figure him out, to see if she could trust him.

Don't bet on it, Connor thought. He took her brush and without touching her painting moved the brush back and forth, demonstrating how to effect roundness and depth, then handed it back.

Connor prided himself on having principles, at least in the classroom, where he long ago had made a rule for himself not to touch his students' work, not to violate their sense of ownership of their painting. It needed to be theirs, Connor knew, no matter how flawed it might be.

His principles became less rigid and more shaky, it had turned out, when he was outside the classroom. Not often, but one indiscretion had been enough—the wrong move at the wrong time, for which he was still paying the price. Now, from this distance in place and time he could see how it had happened, and even be philosophical about it. But none of the other players in that mini-drama was willing to judge the messy situation with Connor's detachment.

Then, out of nowhere, it seemed, Rafael was beside him. Connor had been lost, staring at the pyramid of fruit on the table while his mind wandered. Connor had no idea how long Rafael had been quietly standing there, but Maggie brought him back.

"Connor," she whispered, and pointed towards Rafael with her brush. "Time to rejoin the world." Maggie turned again to her easel, but Connor caught the trace of a smile that played across her lips. Pretty, he thought. Clever, too. Not bad at all.

Rafael leaned in close. "Señora Velez is in the gallery," he whispered. "She wants to see you."

"Now?" Connor asked. Rafael nodded. "She said if you can, please."

Connor stood up and looked around the room. "Okay," he said, "Now try to complete this still life, even if it's rough. But try to capture its essence, if you can. Work on general shapes. Work around the highlights." Eduardo groaned, but Connor ignored him. "I have to go, but I shouldn't be long. Business, you know. Keep working. We'll critique tomorrow." And he followed Rafael out into the courtyard.

Connor knew that Señora Velez never said, "If you can, please," the way Rafael had. No way. That was Rafael softening her words in his gracious Mexican manner. Señora Velez was much too direct for those sorts of niceties. She ran the gallery and this fall workshop in a no-nonsense way. For her, it was art for the peso's sake.

For this was all she had—her husband of thirty-something years died, the story goes, after she earlier had given him hell for spending too much time in Del Jardín on the zócalo sipping *café con leche* and ogling the gringa tourists. That's how he got some time away from her, and that's the last thing he did before walking back up the hill and falling dead.

Señora Velez wouldn't come up to Connor's armpits, and was a few years older, but Connor hadn't felt such a need to say, "Yes ma'am, no ma'am," since the third grade.

What could this be about? Connor wondered. Surely not that he showed up to teach fifteen minutes late, or that he had crept up the stairs after one o'clock last night. Maybe Señora Velez had gotten wind of his suspension back at the university in Texas. Or maybe Mexico had instigated affirmative action or hired Gloria Steinem to vet all teaching appointments. Who the hell could know?

In the art gallery Rafael stepped to one side and eased back out the door, leaving Connor face-to-face with Señora Velez and some other, attractive, woman. Señora Velez nodded towards Connor, introducing him. "This is Señora Lowry, from your state of Colorado."

Connor nodded.

The woman extended her hand with a flash of red fingernails, and gave Connor's hand a firm shake. "Just Ginger," she said.

"Just Connor." He nodded again.

"Señora Lowry is also an artist," Señora Velez explained. "A printmaker,

72

as you can see." She pointed across the room where a series of matted lithographs were propped against the wall. "I plan to show her work in December." Then Señora Velez stopped for a moment. "Or perhaps we could include her prints in your show, in November. A two-artist show. Perhaps that would work better."

"Sounds difficult to me," Connor said. "We already have plans for my opening—a one-man show, you told me—and now with my students' work maybe included, well, her work could get lost, you know."

Señora Velez frowned. "We'll see, we'll see."

Connor shrugged. You can damned sure bet we will, he thought. Then he moved toward the wall and looked more closely at Ginger's prints. He bent down with his hands on his knees. The lithographs were bright, they were bold, they contained all sorts of Mexican iconography—masks and birds and jaguars. Even the ex-convento up Alcalá. There were market stalls overflowing with peppers and flowers, and a burro on a mountain trail.

Several of the prints held an image of the Virgin of Guadalupe, obviously the theme Ginger used to hold the work together as a series. The prints were technically sound and well executed. But terribly commercial. Just what Señora Velez would appreciate, Connor knew. He straightened up.

"Well, Professor Connor, what do you think?" Señora Velez beamed.

"Where in Colorado are you from?" Connor asked, looking straight at Ginger.

"Boulder," she said, with a toss of her head. "At the university. But recently in Aspen." She turned to Señora Velez, as if she wanted her support, then quickly back to Connor. Her hair gleamed red and thick, permed and frizzed, parted down the middle, and cropped bluntly so that it bounced when she moved. She wore jeans and huaraches and a pullover Mexican blouse with embroidered birds soaring around the neck. "The past couple of years in Aspen I taught at the institute there. I've taken a few months off, a sabbatical of sorts."

A sabbatical of sorts, Connor thought. Yeah, a leave of absence without pay. She was in Oaxaca, then, for the same reason he was here, trying to make a few bucks so she could get by for a while.

"Well, these are quite fine," Connor said, turning back to the prints. "I see you've been in Mexico long enough to find some images. It doesn't bother you to borrow the Virgin of Guadalupe for your work?" Connor asked, then immediately regretted it. When he painted here he borrowed from the local culture, too. When you got right down to it we human beings could claim anything and everything, he knew, simply because we could really claim as ours nothing at all.

"The Virgin of Guadalupe is not an 'idea,' Mr. Connor." Her blue eyes flashed. "It is an object, has been objectified by the Mexican people over the centuries, and is there for anyone to appreciate. It has entered the social consciousness in so many ways that it is now universally owned. You appropriate Mexico's flowers, their mountains, their cathedrals, don't you? What would you do? Assassinate my imagination?"

"Okay, okay." Connor shrugged. "I get your point."

But Ginger wasn't finished. "No, I work with what moves me, what speaks to me. Cultural or national boundaries are irrelevant. It's really quite simple if you don't try to over-intellectualize everything."

"Okay, okay," he said again. "I concede your point."

Señora Velez stepped between them, facing Connor, who backed a couple of steps away. "Señora Lowry has come to ask a favor," she said. "And I told her, Profesor Connor, that you would be happy to cooperate." Not a question at all.

Connor nodded. "I'm sure," he said. But what kind of favor, he wondered. He glanced at his watch.

"You need to get back," Ginger said. "You're teaching, I understand. I'll walk with you and maybe I can explain." She thanked Señora Velez and led the way out into the courtyard. "I meant for this to be so easy," Ginger said, glancing back over her shoulder. "But you know Señora Velez. The way she has to run everything."

They stopped in the shade of the balcony, and both watched Rafael at the far end of the courtyard as he chopped apples and oranges into bite-sized chunks and fed the macaws. "You'll meet Rafael," Connor said. "He's a great guy."

Ginger flushed and tossed her head. "No," she said. "I mean, yes. I met him the other day. He is a great guy. Nice, you know. And smart."

Connor nodded. Lately there had always seemed to be another man who was younger and smarter. Maybe nicer. He thought about his soon-to-be ex-wife Jean and her new man, William Bones. Younger? Yeah, a little, maybe. Smarter? Connor wasn't ready to concede that, but some days he wondered.

"Yeah, Rafael's smart. Smart enough, I hope," Connor said, "to stay out of trouble."

Ginger looked startled. "What sort of trouble do you mean?"

"Politics, you know. All the demonstrations and protests. The cops here in Oaxaca—well, they're not a bunch of Mr. Sensitives. And the mayor and governor won't back down." Connor glanced back at Rafael. "He just needs to watch his step."

"Just a minute," she said, "I'll be right back," and she hurried out toward Rafael.

Connor moved over and leaned against a stone column. From there he watched Ginger as she said something to Rafael that made him laugh. She wore hiking shorts that came down almost to her knees. Ginger's arms were pale, with traces of freckles. A redhead's skin.

In a few moments Ginger was back next to Connor, not making eye contact with him, looking a little flushed. She kicked off her sandals. They were new, locally made from recycled tires—Connor had passed mounds of them at the Abastos market. "These are killing me," she complained. "I thought my feet would adjust, but I don't think I can last that long." She laughed, rubbing the soles of her feet on the grass that Rafael kept clipped short. "But everything handmade isn't wonderful. And I guess you get what you pay for. Lesson number sixty-six from Mexico."

"How long have you been here?" Connor asked. "Sixty-six. That's lots of lessons."

"Four long weeks," Ginger said with a slight grimace.

Connor grinned. "I understand. I sure understand. So what can I do for you?"

Ginger told him straight-out, with no apologies. "I need to sit in on your classes. I'm scheduled to teach watercolor, for God's sake, at the Aspen Institute next spring. A six-week session to a bunch of women coming in from the East Coast. Watercolor. That's one thing I've never conquered." She stopped a moment to see if Connor was with her. "I'm a printmaker. That's something I know. And a painter—acrylics and oils. No problem. But watercolor? Not the best thing I've ever done. And to tell the truth—and this is between us—I need the money. The institute offered me the class, so I accepted."

"I think I'm beginning to get the picture," Connor volunteered. "So you need to brush up on technique?"

"Right," she said, "and I can watercolor enough to get by. I took a class in grad school, but I've forgotten how to talk about the medium. I mean the language of criticism, how to handle that kind of class."

"Sure," Connor said. "Sit in. We're there three mornings a week, nine to noon, or a little after. Sometimes a short field trip."

"I can't pay," she said, looking a little pathetic. "I can't afford it."

Connor wanted to say, "Well, hell lady, I'm not doing this for grins." But he held back. "Don't worry about it. Maybe you can return the favor in some way." Ah, Connor, he thought. You're irredeemably bad.

For a minute Connor could see Ginger going back over what he had said. She frowned, and crossed her arms under her breasts. She looked Connor in the eye. He felt her start to strike back in some way, but then she seemed to let it pass.

"I mean, maybe I could watch you pull some prints, or something," he said.

She nodded. "Okay. Friday then? At nine?"

"Just remember that it's my class, that you're my guest, and it'll work. Okay?"

"Hey," Ginger shot back. "I'm not that pushy." She laughed. "Although a couple of men in my past have more than hinted otherwise. But I'll watch myself. I promise." She turned to move away, then stopped. "I'm sorry about that little lecture I gave you, that appropriation bullshit. I'll be honest. I've been making art since I was sixteen—a long time—and I have a storage unit full of the stuff. I'm ready to make art that will sell, and when in Mexico—well, you know. Señora Velez likes what I'm doing, and what she likes she can sell. When she sells I get paid. It's really quite simple."

"Well, I was out of line," Connor admitted, "saying what I did. All that academic stuff does get in the way." He stopped for a moment. "And I figure I'm pretty well done with academia, myself."

Ginger looked surprised. "Why is that? I figured you were the last bastion of the academy."

"A long story," Connor said. "A long, and so far, a sad story."

Ginger reached out and touched his arm. "I'd like to hear," she said. "When we both have time." And Connor hoped she meant it.

The class was breaking up when Connor finally got back, and he waited, busying himself with pretend paperwork while the students packed their things and cleaned their brushes in the wall-hung sink.

Maggie was the last to leave, her canvas bag over her shoulder. Conner shoved his chair back and they walked across the courtyard together.

"Where you headed?" Connor asked as they reached the sidewalk in front of the gallery.

"Oh," she said. "Yesterday I dropped off some film at the camera store. It's just the other side of the zócalo."

"Well I'm headed to Del Jardín for more coffee and maybe an early lunch. Why don't you stop back by? Join me. My treat."

Maggie laughed, then wagged her head side to side. "Why not?" She glanced up at the dark clouds gathering above. "Well, I'd better get moving or I may get wet. I won't be long."

It had rained almost every afternoon in early October, the fault of El Niño, everyone said. And some late-season unisex-named hurricane had skirted the Baja and filled the atmosphere that unloaded on the Oaxacan valley when the heat built up. Now only a spatter of drops followed what had been a quick-moving rain shower.

In Del Jardín Maggie looked around for Connor. He wasn't there. Maybe I misunderstood him, Maggie thought. Or probably, he's just an artist and not too reliable. I'd better watch my step. Oh, well, I'll wait fifteen minutes. She found a table under the overhang, slid her sack of slides between her feet, motioned for a waiter, and ordered a café con leche. She took her camera from around her neck and placed it on the table next to her purse with its strap looped around a table leg and watched the rain come in, scattering the tourists.

Finally Connor, with a sheepish look on his face, wandered into Del Jardín. He pulled up a chair, his hair and shoulders damp from the rain. "This vendor," he said. "An old guy. I felt sorry for him. He had leather vests his wife had made. I must have tried on half a dozen. All way too small. Sorry I'm late."

Maggie shrugged and shook her head side to side. Just another man, she thought.

Where Connor and Maggie sat they faced the zócalo and watched the street. Some years before, vehicle traffic was banned from the streets that circled the plaza and now people scurried by, shaking the water from bright pieces of plastic they had held over their heads, stepping around puddles of rainwater that had collected from the sudden shower. But now, with the rain passing to the north, vendors had begun to cart their goods from under sheltered overhangs and back out onto the cobblestone streets.

Connor ordered a Negra Modelo. "Too late for coffee," he said, glancing up at the TV, and then they talked, Connor mostly asking questions, starting with, "Why are you here?"

"I'm a photographer," Maggie said. "A photographer primarily, but a writer, of sorts, too. At least I document the photographs I take. Oaxaca is one fine place to be working."

Connor motioned towards her camera. "An OM1," he said with a nod of approval. "But not digital? I thought film was becoming obsolete."

Maggie laughed. "Not for me, not yet. Film, black and white mostly. That's how I learned; that's what I know. And what I still love." She took a sip of coffee. "And film? Yeah, it may fade away, but I don't think it will disappear. And here, in Mexico, film is still everywhere. In the cities, at least."

While they talked the zócalo came alive, soon thick with plastic blow-up toys, ducks and alligators and dogs and rockets and balloons. On one corner a man pulled purple ears of steaming corn from a black pot. He impaled them on sticks, slathered the corn with globs of butter and sprinkled them with red chile.

Young girls with practiced pitiful frowns stopped at their table and pushed tiny braided bracelets at them. Old women wandered by with weathered faces and open palms. A blind accordion player sang mournful Mexican songs while a slight girl slipped between tables holding out a tin can. Connor slid a few coins in change from the slick-topped table where they sat and dropped them into the can.

"You can't feed them all," Maggie said with a smile.

"Just buying off my guilt."

"Guilt?" Maggie asked. "For what?"

"You name it," Connor said, and they both laughed. He felt at ease now, here on the plaza with this woman.

To Connor Maggie appeared to be the kind of woman who wouldn't at this time in her life be bothered with pretensions, for she wore nothing to flatter herself, no makeup to speak of, no permed and frizzed hair. Her only nod to adornment was the two simple silver hoops that dangled from her pierced ears. She sat there at Del Jardín like a woman who knew what she was about, by all appearances, a woman who had come to know herself in the '70s and had stayed there, more or less, a part of those times, but never dared to act out what she knew then, until now.

Connor had already given Maggie a fifteen-minute recap of his life, the pasteurized, abridged version for sure, leaving in the divorce from Jean, leaving out the complications with that graduate student. He skipped over the fact that he had no job to return to, describing his time here in Oaxaca as a sabbatical. You give people what they expect and want to hear, Connor thought. It's so much simpler that way.

Now he followed up on his question to Maggie, which had been a routine, "Why are you here?" sort of query. The expected question but with an unexpected answer, the "I'm a photographer." Connor wanted more. "Okay, you're a photographer, but that covers lots of territory. Subject matter? People, churches, markets—lots of possibilities here."

"Actually most people might think that what I do is gross," Maggie said, with a wag of her head and a glance around Del Jardín. She paused. "I photograph amputees."

Connor raised his eyebrows, took a sip of beer.

"All sorts," she continued. "With whatever, arms, legs, hands, ears, noses missing. And Mexico's a great place to find them, especially here in the south, especially in the little pueblos where they farm." She stopped, thought she might have gone too far, but Connor leaned forward, making a circular motion with one hand along with a nod, signaling her to go on.

"I talk to them—they're mostly men. Those who will pose for me, letting me photograph everything, their cuts, the scars, what is missing, and then I record their stories." Maggie reached down to tap a small bag, one that Connor guessed probably held a micro recorder. "It's really not that hard once you get into it. And they don't seem to mind. Actually it may be a way to acknowledge, and accept, what happened." She shrugged. "Or maybe I just rationalize that."

Connor leaned back in his chair. "Well, I never would have guessed." What he would have guessed the first day he met Maggie was this is another middle-aged woman down in Oaxaca on a lark, maybe bored, or maybe a divorcee blowing her alimony.

"How long have you been doing this?" Connor asked. "How long in Mexico?"

"Long enough so that I may never go back," she said, and looked around, past the cathedral across the way, all the way to the small rise of mountains that stretched into the clouds way west of the city. "And long enough so that I'm not sure where home is."

She turned back to Connor. "Do you ever get homesick?"

"Homesick? I hadn't thought about it," he said. Although he knew he had. "So I guess not." You must have had a home to get homesick, Connor figured, and Abilene was never that. But he did think about earlier days, hanging around Austin, mostly faking his way through grad school. The closest place to home since high school.

Connor tossed some peanuts across the stone walkway, and watched the pigeons flutter and scramble and fuss. "I get a little homesick, I guess. Some things I miss, about Austin mostly." But he knew that wasn't homesickness, but time sickness. Not just to be back there, to a place that had changed almost beyond recognition, but to be there and young again and do things over, this time right.

"But I'm more interested in what you're doing with those photographs. And especially why? For a book? But amputees? Why, for God's sake?" He waited, squeezing a little lime into the last of his beer. He noted the color of the lime, in Mexico a *limone*, small, smooth, yellow-green. He would have his students try to capture that color next week in class.

Maggie fidgeted with her camera strap. She looked at Connor in a puzzled sort of way.

Connor felt her hesitation. "Maybe I'm being too pushy," he volunteered.

"No, it's all right." Maggie seemed a long way off to Connor, and then suddenly felt very close. "There are reasons," she said, "for what I am doing. It has to do with my mother, I think. I'll try to explain it sometime, before too long, if you want to hear."

She caught Connor's eyes, trying to figure him out. Was this a man she could trust? Only one way to know. "I'm going out tomorrow, east past Tlacalula, then down in the valley to the south. There's a scattering of pueblos there, strung out along a little stream. They grow lots of corn, some alfalfa for hay, I understand."

"They drink a lot of mezcal?" Connor asked. "And swing a lot of sharp machetes?"

Maggie gave a little laugh and shook her head. "Well, maybe. Anyway, my source here in Oaxaca, a doctor, tells me I should go." She pushed back her chair and stood. "Why don't you come along?"

Maggie felt herself flush when she asked, felt adolescent again in a little rush that she quickly moved beyond. She checked the strap of her camera again, and fingered a rough spot where the leather had frayed.

Connor shrugged. Tomorrow was Saturday and he had no plans. "You have a car?" He didn't want to split taxi fare for a fifty-mile round trip, or bounce on some third-class bus for a couple of hours. He's had enough of Mexican buses to last for the duration. He would fly out of Mexico when he left, or, by God, he would stay.

"A car of sorts," Maggie said with a laugh. "An old Blazer. You'll know you've had a ride. It needs new shocks, or maybe fewer Mexican roads. Anyway, it should get us there and back."

"What time in the morning?" Connor asked.

"Is early okay? Eight, eight-thirty?"

Connor nodded. "Whenever you say. It will be my pleasure."

Maggie extended her hand as if to seal the agreement. Connor took it with a grin. She looked at him, his fair skin, the traces of sun damage on his forehead. His face was angular, a little too bony to be outright handsome, and today, in the bright sun, he appeared gaunt, as if something Maggie didn't know had been pulling him down.

"You have a hat?" she asked, realizing that something about Connor brought out her maternal instincts. Not good, but she would watch it. "A lot more sun than shade around these villages. Centuries of firewood gathering, you know. It's best to wear a hat." Oh, damn, she thought. Why can't I just leave the poor man alone? This is probably the sort of Mom thing that drove Kelly away.

"I've been meaning to pick one up," Connor said. "Should have long ago. I'll check out the *mercado* later. And I'll be right here in the morning, finishing up my *huevos* and coffee, ready for action."

Maggie leaned over to unwind the camera strap from the chair and with one finger checked the top button of her blouse. "Bring a sketch book, a camera, whatever you like. And some water."

Connor nodded and Maggie grabbed her bag and turned away, striding quickly across the street of river stone. Connor watched her, the way she moved with what he saw as practiced self-assurance, an assurance that seemed paradoxically to compensate for something she must have lost. In a moment she vanished into the now-crowded zócalo.

Before she rounded the corner Maggie glanced back at Connor. Oh, God, she thought. Why did I do that? I was doing just fine on my own. She made her way down the side of the *alameda*, stopping for a moment to inspect some carved, brightly painted wooden figures. She picked one up, a devil man with an exaggerated evil scowl, holding a bottle of tequila. The vendor quickly gave her the price, but she shook her head. "I may already have one of these," she said, "And one may be more than plenty."

Back at Del Jardín Connor motioned for the check. He slid his chair around so that he could scan the zócalo, where Maggie had disappeared. A little adventure, he thought. With a woman. Not his first choice, and an image of Ginger Lowry came to him, the way she had worked at painting today, losing herself in that simple still life, quickly covering the paper with color, and then even more quickly ripping it off her pad and starting over again. Everything Ginger did seemed impetuous. She had rushed out right after class as if she had to be somewhere important. Connor hoped she wasn't avoiding him.

After he paid for the drinks Connor sat alone at the table, watching the passing parade of people, feeling the energy, the life on the street before him. A solitary man with a saxaphone swayed in the cobblestone street. A few random notes cut through the air, as if the musician were searching for something, the right place to begin. Finally the notes came together and he played the same tune he did every day. He didn't play well, the notes a little flat in places, and the song was sad and plaintive. But the man played with feeling, and Connor found himself humming along. Finally, the words came to him, and he sang along, mostly mouthing the lyrics to "With a Song in My Heart," until Connor laughed out loud. But he knew there were worse things than a man having a song in his heart.

CHAPTER 11

In the village of Santa Maria del Rio, Maggie took charge. Her source, Dr. Reyes in Oaxaca, had been right, and after less than an hour she had three scarred men, half-naked, backed up against the side wall of an adobe shed. Quickly she had shot two rolls of film. She loaded the camera once more, only now aware of the sprinkling of villagers who had gathered to watch, and once again aware of Connor, the way he held back from the others.

With a smile she noted that he wore a new *campesino* straw hat for protection from the Oaxacan sun, the hat pulled so low the brim almost touched his dark glasses. He seemed outlandishly tall there in the pueblo, where all the men looked up even to Maggie. Connor leaned against the peeling bark of an ancient cottonwood tree and sipped a can of Modelo, camouflaged by the splatter of light and shadow that filtered through the leaves.

Maggie pulled the camera to her eye and panned left to right, watching the needle of the light meter as it fluctuated, a little too wildly, and she made a mental note to change the battery. While she worked with the camera, aproned women gathered behind her in a semicircle, joined now by a few men who squatted on their haunches in that typical campesino way of waiting and watching. Children played along the dirt trail that led by the shed on its worn way from the village to the stream that meandered below. The dust they made lifted in the air, slowly fell, and settled to the west where the light wind pushed it with soft gusts.

Then for her that world vanished, and once again Maggie knew only the men and the rawness of their stumps. She tried to imagine the stories that they would tell from the scars on their bodies, the stories they would later speak into her tape recorder that hung in its case that Connor kept for her, slung over his shoulder.

Earlier, each of the three men had been summoned by the village elder, and each one in his own time came to Maggie while she waited on a bench in the middle of the small plaza at Santa Maria del Rio. The three men finally gathered there, two walking with the aid of handmade crutches, the arm supports cushioned with wrapped rags. The third man's right arm was missing almost to his shoulder.

The three men had come to Maggie where she waited with one elder of the village who had read Dr. Reyes's letter and given his approval. When he assured them that no harm would come of this, the elder led the three men and Maggie slowly down the hill from the plaza and around a turn in the trail to an adobe house where the elder lived.

Maggie moved around the outside of the house, one eye on shadow and sun, and past a shed whose front wall was lengths of rusted tin. There she checked the angle of the sun once more, and shook her head, then moved around the corner and chose a side wall of the shed. It had at one time been whitewashed and now had faded and would make a neutral backdrop for her photographs.

Maggie gestured that she wanted the men to stand with their backs to the wall. They looked to the elder and he nodded that they should. Maggie would photograph the three men straight on and in focus. Nothing fancy, no arty angles, no soft blurring. No seduction. She takes what the camera sees.

There was a minute of awkwardness as Maggie explained to the elder in Spanish what she wanted. This man, who was probably about Connor's age, walked with a rocking bow-legged gait and spoke his Zapotec words to the three maimed men and they listened and nodded. Then everyone who had gathered there waited in silence.

The man with one arm came around first, began to unbutton his wheat-colored shirt with his one hand, all the time staring, almost glaring, at Maggie. But she neither blinked nor flinched, just stood watching, with her camera hanging heavily from the strap around her neck.

At that moment Maggie felt a tension run through her, and even while she watched that one man with all her concentration she remembered other men, whole men, and other times when shirts were loosened and unbuttoned.

And then suddenly she could see her mother's scars, could feel their roughness as she had soaped and gently scrubbed the flatness of her chest. Maggie felt heavy, and a sigh rose from deep within. For a moment she feared the futility of what she was attempting. Photographing scarred and maimed men would not bring her mother back or erase her mother's suffering. But it might help, in some way that Maggie didn't fully comprehend.

The man with one arm pulled his shirt off and around, wadded the shirt into a ball and tossed it to the side. He stood erect then, his chest bare, rising and falling with the exertion, the stump of his arm a crisscross of scars and folded skin.

Then, and only then it seemed, could the other two men follow. They let their trousers fall to the ground. Both had lost part of their left legs, one below and one just above the knee. The three of them stood quietly, exposing their wounds to Maggie, the gringa lady with the Chevy Blazer and the fast-shooting camera, and to their neighbors and to their kin of the pueblo.

Now Maggie moved closer, the camera clicked, and the motor drive came alive, purred forward, clicked, purred, clicked, purred. Maggie stopped to face the men, not condescending, not with pity in her eyes, but straight on. She looked at them as the men they were. A woman seeing them as three men, then each individually, meeting the first one's eyes, then moving to the next, and then to the next.

Maggie crouched slightly and then quickly dropped to her knees in the dirt. She shot again and again, slowing only to change the lens from 50 to 135 and back. She raced through thirty-six frames in a few quick minutes, the clicking of the camera and the purr of the motor drive the only sounds.

Finally Maggie straightened up and looked around for the elder. "That's good," she said, and the elder nodded and gestured to the men who broke into shy smiles.

For a long time they stayed there, leaning against the whitewashed adobe wall, two with no trousers and long shirts wafting in the light breeze, and the third man with no shirt. All three still wore their crumpled, stained straw hats. The elder spoke a few words to them, then turned to give his approval to Maggie with a slight bow.

Only then did the men pull on their clothes. They followed Maggie back up the trail to the village plaza where they sat on iron benches and sipped Cokes that Maggie brought them from the corner *tienda*.

Maggie pulled the recorder from its case and spoke quietly into it, so quietly that Connor could not catch her words, even though he had joined them at the plaza and had settled onto the shaded steps of the nearby church. Then she held the microphone to the one-armed man and he began to speak, and Connor could pick up the faint song of Zapotec words. Connor sat and watched from the church and downed the last of his warm beer.

Then he stood and rolled the sleeves of his shirt two turns. He stretched, and dark blue circles of sweat showed under his arms. He crushed the Modelo can until it was flat and stuck it in his pocket. Connor shook his head, still amazed by the wonder of what he had seen.

Later, Connor drove the Blazer back toward town, leaning forward to better watch for potholes in the narrow road. He eased the vehicle over rough outcroppings of rocks and across the sandy gravel of dry creek beds. Finally, almost at dark, he found the main highway that led back to Oaxaca. While he drove, Maggie jotted down entries into a notebook, and they did not speak.

There had been a moment, back in the pueblo, when the one-armed man stripped off his shirt that Connor had fought off the urge to move forward and stop Maggie from humiliating that man. He had wanted to shout, "Hell, Maggie, this is Mexico. Let things be, work their own ways out." But soon he realized that he had misread what was happening, and had no way to anticipate what might happen next. So he waited and soon his latent anger turned to disbelief, his disbelief to amazement. "Hell, she's really pulling it off," he had murmured to himself. And then Connor had been freed up to observe, no longer with apprehension or with anger. It was as if this were a healing ceremony and Maggie had transformed herself into a curandera.

And for the first time he had seen Maggie for who she was, a woman, strong and sure, yet calm and compassionate with the three men, and Connor knew he had never been near a woman like Maggie O'Neill.

While Maggie had crouched and knelt and moved to her left and then to her right, with her concentration on the three men, Connor could see that her camera had become an extension of her eye. But more than of her eye. Connor watched as a radiance came over her, a certain intangible sense of sureness, of confidence that seemed to emanate a glow. Something rare.

He thought of Jean, the evening in Abilene at an art opening at a university's small museum, the way her face took on its own special radiance just being in the same room with, Connor later discovered, her new lover, William Bones. Sexual excitement surrounded her, and only a fool would not have seen it, known it.

But this with Maggie today went beyond that, Connor knew. For it was grounded in something far deeper than sexual excitement that would inevitably cool and fade.

Then his mind wandered to Ginger. How on the first day in his watercolor class she had rearranged the still life he had set up, saying it was too symmetrical. He remembered how she bristled when Eduardo challenged her in class over something insignificant.

She never could have handled something like this today, not the way Maggie did. Ginger would have let her ego interfere, been way too self-conscious about her looks and worried how she might be perceived by these strange men. Ginger would have turned it all into performance art, about her, with the village her stage, and the maimed men merely her props.

Connor glanced over at Maggie, who all this while had struggled to write in her notebook despite the rough road, uncomplaining as the Blazer bounced its way back to Oaxaca. In the last glow of light Connor could see the possibility that she might be a *bruja* of sorts. No, he thought, she's much too straightforward for that. She's not even a crystal gazer. But he figured, with a slight smile, that he'd better watch his step around this one.

With a sigh, Maggie dropped the notebook beside her on the seat. She wiped the camera lens and labeled the canisters of film. Finally, she turned to Connor.

"Thanks for driving," she said with a shake of her head. "And thanks for going with me. Sorry it took so long." She leaned toward her open window and let the dry air rush across her face and whip through her hair.

"No problem," he said with a glance her way. "My pleasure, for sure. Makes me thankful to be only a painter of pretty scenes." He shook his head. "I don't see how you can keep that up week after week."

"Well, they don't all go this well—some don't even go at all. The older fellow, the elder, was the key, he and the doctor in town. If not for them I'd have come up empty."

But Connor had seen her work, sensed her determination, and figured she hardly ever came up empty. What Maggie did went way beyond ordinary art. Her photographs, the whole process with the men, made his landscapes and still lifes, as well executed as they might be, seem trivial. How could he go back to still more of the same, the ordinary paintings that he pulled off without much effort and zero emotion week after week. For what? He had boxes of them in a storage unit in Texas, and now in Mexico had completed several more. Señora Velez would be lucky to sell two or three at the opening in November, and Connor would have the leftovers in another box that he would slide under his bed.

"You have time for a drink?" he asked. "And some dinner? I'm starved." He switched on the Blazer's headlights, concentrating on the traffic now that they reached the edge of the city.

"Sure," Maggie said. "That sounds fine. But maybe I'll stop by my hotel if it's all right. These khakis." She brushed at the knees. "I need to change."

Connor stopped at a red light just then and a boy, hardly even a teenager, hurried into the road in front of them. He held a lit torch above his head waving it back and forth to get their attention, then quickly took a sip from a bottle in his other hand. He tilted his head back and blew across the torch into the darkening sky. The flame roared, shooting out six or eight feet, and the boy sipped again and blew across the torch once more. Then with a grin on his face and his hand out he began to work the cars lined up at the red light.

"Suck that in instead of out," Connor said, "and 'boom' there go the lungs."

"Oh, my God," Maggie said. "He'll kill himself," and quickly dug into the backpack for her coin purse. She found a few pesos and held them out the open window. The light turned green and the boy raced around in front of the Blazer. A taxi behind them honked. "Just a damned minute," Connor said, glaring into the rearview mirror.

The boy reached for the coins, but Maggie grabbed his hand. In her quick Spanish she told him that the pesos were his only if he promised never to do the flame-blowing stunt again. "You must promise," she said. "Please."

With a grin the boy nodded his agreement, took the pesos and hurried to the edge of the road.

Connor gunned the Blazer and they took off. Half a block away Connor checked his rearview mirror and spotted a flame shooting across the sky.

CHAPTER 12

Connor dropped Maggie by Las Golondrinas, left the Blazer parked on the street, and made his way the few blocks back downtown. He found an empty outside table at Del Jardín and spotted his usual waiter. He gave Connor a grin and nodded. In a couple of minutes Connor had a cold Dos Equis and a shot of mezcal in front of him.

The waiter left a menu on the table. Connor glanced through it and decided on a Cubana sandwich. He set the menu aside and waited. Maggie had said just a few minutes, but it didn't matter. He had no reason to hurry.

Connor sipped the mezcal, chased it with the beer, and slowly things lightened up. He thought back on the day with Maggie and for the first time in years he felt fresh, almost young again. He found himself excited in some vague sort of way, anticipating what might happen next, and out of nowhere a whole new idea for his watercolors came to mind. Maybe he could take off on Maggie's photographs and come up with a series of paintings that wouldn't be meant to please, but instead would startle and disturb. That's what he had been missing. Good art should disturb at some level; he knew that intellectually, but over the years he had become lazy, indifferent. He had taken the easy way for too many years. Maybe he and Maggie could collaborate on a book, his watercolors juxtaposed with her photographs. Maybe . . .

and suddenly he knew what he had been missing. He had forgotten how to dream, and without dreams life can be miserable. He shook his head, amazed at how fine he felt, and a grin slid across his face.

Connor stretched back in the metal chair. He dug deep in his pocket for coins and emptied a handful on the table. The coins were all sizes, some the old pesos, big and heavy and practically worthless, and some new, with their bands of silver around centers of brass. Even now, after living in Oaxaca for several weeks, he had a hard time getting the coins straight, so as best he could he put them in equal stacks, ending up with a circle of seven stacks which he covered with his hat. Tonight he would say yes to those who wandered by his table with Chiclets or an off-key song or carved wooden spoons and combs. He would say yes to the hands that reached out, the old, withered, slack-skinned hands, and the eager, young, dirty hands. Tonight Connor wanted to say yes to everything.

In her hotel room Maggie tossed her dusty clothes to one side and stood in the shower without moving. Her thoughts rambled in and out of the day, second-guessing what she'd said, what she'd done; an old bad habit. For the first time she could remember, her body had a smell. From the hot afternoon of work or from the kilometers back to town in the over-heated Blazer, perhaps. But this smell seemed different, more elemental, an almost animal odor that came from somewhere within, something that had come alive again and startled her. Maggie turned the shower all the way up until it steamed. The spray stung her body. She soaped and shampooed to wash the smell away. She thought of Connor, waiting at Del Jardín, probably, surely, on his second beer by now. Maggie stepped out of the shower and grabbed a towel. She needed to hurry.

But Maggie stood at the curtained window of her room and dried herself with the thin towel. Clean clothes felt marvelous. She pulled the curtain back. The lights from the city glowed above the trees. What if Connor hadn't waited; had already left? No, she thought, if for no other reason he has my Blazer keys. He'll be there.

Later, at Del Jardín, Connor finished off his Cubana sandwich while Maggie sipped on her second glass of Mexican red wine and nibbled on a crispy torta. Now Connor had his straw hat back on his head, the stacks of coins long since no longer on the table. For the past thirty minutes they had talked, and now grew quiet and watched the nightly strolling around the zócalo.

Connor lost himself while going through their time there together, just talking. This is what you do, he thought, when you get to know someone new. You reveal your past, a little at a time, you invent and then reinvent your history to suit the occasion, to fit your perception of your life that is most appropriate for the moment. That's not a bad thing, but a natural way of being, disclosing, a way men and women had of moving along somewhat upright, with a little dignity, instead of being on all fours, braying as they went. Or wriggling around on their bellies.

We all did it, Connor knew, it was part of the human dance, the self-explanation and self-delusion that allowed us to get up each new morning and hit the streets again.

He had drifted off into his own private world and caught himself when Maggie shifted in her chair and spoke again, picking back up where she had fallen silent earlier. He nodded and leaned toward her.

"You asked about Kelly. He's a sweet boy," Maggie said. "Sensitive. Not like his dad at all. Last I heard from him he was excited to be working with leather, making belts and sandals and even hats. He's learned it all from some old fellow in Taos."

"A sweet boy, you said?" Connor asked. "How old is he?"

"Well, not exactly a boy." Maggie took another sip of wine. "He's a man, I guess. He was twenty-four in July. But still always my boy."

"That's a man," Connor said. "Anyway at twenty-four I was a man, already a father. Not that I'd recommend that. In those days it just seemed to happen." He laughed and saw the smile in Maggie's eyes. He liked the way she understood things. A lot different from the younger gals he had spent time with.

"And Claire?" Maggie asked. "She's, what did you say? Also twenty-four?"

Connor grinned and leaned forward in his chair. He lifted his Dos Equis to make a toast, noticed the bottle was drained, and reached for his shot glass of tequila. He nodded. "Yeah, twenty-four. Well, I guess we were up to the same thing about twenty-four years ago." He laughed, a fresh disarming laugh.

A laugh that's for me, Maggie thought, full of practiced charm. Connor lifted the glass and Maggie noticed the way he held it, with two slender fingers and his thumb, the other two fingers held back in a delicate sort of way. He's not the ruffian he pretends to be, Maggie thought.

"And here's to another twenty-four years, by God!" Connor tossed back what was left of the tequila and Maggie raised her wine glass. "Why not?" she said with a smile. "I'll drink to that." She took another sip of wine and felt a small, involuntary shiver, but hid it by shifting in her chair.

"Can I ask you a question?" Connor looked straight across the table at her. Maggie shrugged. "I guess so. Sure."

"Yesterday, when you first told me about your project, you said sometime you would explain why you were doing this. You said something about your mother, but it was awfully vague."

"Vague, yes, probably because I'm still struggling with it. But if you're sure you want to hear this sad story, I'll try."

"It wouldn't be the first sad story I've heard," Connor said. "And probably not the last."

So Maggie leaned close and spoke softly. Her mother had been manic-depressive all of her adult life, so when Maggie escaped the tumult of her home she stayed away. College not quite completed, she latched on to Gordon. Then Kelly came along, and she mostly kept her mother out of her new life. "Daddy had cut and run years before, but that's another sad story I'll skip for now."

"You go ahead, it's your story," Connor could tell this was important to Maggie. "I'm listening."

She told what she could, what she could remember, all in a stream that seemed beyond her control.

"Mama lived outside of Houston in one of those towns that had been overrun by the city's growth, an hour's drive away. There were our occasional, sudden visits that invariably ended with me afterwards all emotional and angry and swearing never to go through that again. She was, I figure, undiagnosed manic-depressive. Just impossible for me.

"Then out of nowhere came her cancer diagnosis, and the medical center in Houston, near where I lived, seemed the best option, so . . ." and Maggie got quiet for a moment.

"Well, I found a room for her in an assisted care home nearby. Surgery followed surgery, time dragged on, and each time I was there, helping the poor attendants with the bathing and changing dressings and then forcing myself to give comfort as best I could. The conflicts between us never went away, were never resolved; sadness and anger between us until the end."

Maggie sighed and leaned back in her chair, visibly drained. "I'm sorry.

I went on and on. But I gave a lot in those two years, and ended up losing a mother, a not-so-good marriage, and almost losing a quite-fine son. That's it, I guess."

Connor shook his head. "A damned sad story for sure," he said. "I'm sorry."

"Thanks for asking—and for listening." Maggie needed to take this somewhere else. "Now let me ask you something."

"Uh-oh," Connor said. "This could get tricky."

Maggie smiled. "This isn't as heavy. I'm just curious what you thought, today, seeing those men with their stumps and their scars? You know, exposed like that." Maggie wasn't sure where her motive for asking came from. A need for confirmation, or from her insecurity, or maybe a need for her project to be validated. Or, perhaps, wanting to better understand this strange man seated across from her. Maggie sat back and waited.

Connor thought a minute. He studied Maggie and tried to see beyond the mask of her face. He sensed that for more than one reason this was an important question. Flip, deflective easy answers snapped through his mind, but went no further.

For a moment he put himself back in that village, watching the men struggle up that trail, still fully clothed, their missing limbs obvious. Then the three of them backed up against the wall.

"My first thought," he said, "probably because of my life's experiences, was what can these men do, no longer able to farm or find other work in any meaningful way. How can they continue to support their families? I doubt that the Mexican government offered more than token help, maybe only at first, after the immediate medical stuff that kept them alive.

"And sure," he said, "I'll be honest with you. It bothered me." Connor took a deep breath. "And I'm not all that squeamish. But it didn't bother me the way I would have imagined. Maybe it was how the men did it, the way they exposed their wounds, their losses, with that anger and defiance at first, and then at the end with that enormous, final relief. That jolted me. I guess all of that together somehow made it okay." Connor shrugged. "Okay for them, how things worked out, and also for me. But that's not an easy question to answer."

He leaned forward again, waited for the adjoining table of tourists to ease by and move on. He spoke quietly. "It seems that if things bother you or not depends on the context, the way you feel things are handled. And I think you pulled it off in spades."

"Oops," he said, sensing a need to back off. "There. I used that feel word. I'd better watch out or I'll slide into dangerous territory." Connor laughed then, a release from the tension he'd built up.

"Just a minute," he said. "I'll be right back. Too many beers. The Caballeros room is calling." He slid his chair back from the table and stood. He rubbed his butt. "Damn these metal chairs," he said with a grimace. He touched the brim of his hat and moved away.

Maggie smiled. He's almost quaint, she thought, as she watched Connor make his way back through the crowded tables and disappear through the swinging doors, maybe even courtly in a southern gentlemanly way that didn't bother her. Maggie noted Connor's good points: a sensitive and sympathetic listener, intelligent, talented, an entertaining sense of humor, tall, nice-enough looking. He has a grown daughter, so he's survived life with a teenager. He seems sincere and well-intentioned—up to some yet unknown point.

Then quickly she inventoried the downside: too self-centered (were all men?), drinks too much, has an eye for younger women (she thought of Ginger Lowry), and his years and his miles are easy to see. He's lost contact with his daughter for some reason, and he seems to want to do the right thing more than he does it.

A washout, she thought. Not a good long-term risk, probably, but long-term wasn't what Maggie was about, anyway. Except with her photography, the only commitment she cared about, at least for now.

Connor worked his way back to where Maggie waited, picking his path around the chairs and tables, crowded with tourists. The noise had raised a level or two, and he could make out a little German and some French. A Brit, or probably an Aussie, was mouthing off in one corner. One table of Texans he had spotted early on, talking loud about Lubbock and how they would be in Red River skiing for Christmas. He made a wide circle around them.

Connor stopped just before he reached their table and watched Maggie. She was staring out across the zócalo deep into her own thoughts, it seemed. Then she ran her finger lightly around of the rim of her wine glass, and from where he stood he could just pick up the high-pitched sound it made.

When she turned his way, her eyes were soft and in the overhead lights, more green than brown. Maggie seemed to glow and possessed an attraction that Connor couldn't quite define. She gave him a quick, bright smile and he eased back down in the metal chair. She ran her finger around the wine glass again until it rang. She held her hand above the glass for a moment, then silenced it with a light touch.

"Good hands," Connor said. He took her hand then and lightly kissed her fingers. "Saw that once in a foreign film," he said, and Maggie laughed.

"You're a real gentleman, Connor. I can tell."

"Well, seriously now. You know what? I like you. I think you're a terrific woman."

Maggie flushed, tried to pull her hand back, but he held on. "You're sweet, Connor. And I like you, but . . ."

"It's settled then," Connor said with a laugh. "Hey, that's a pretty good start. I like you and you like me. Not bad at all." He leaned towards her. "I could ask you to go dancing, I guess. Or maybe we could skip that, and I could invite you up to my room to see my watercolors. Hmmm. But you've already seen some of them. The view from the balcony is great at night, though. And you haven't seen that."

Connor squeezed her hand and let it go. He scratched at the label of his empty beer bottle. Then he looked up again. "I'm not very good at this, I guess. Out of practice. Maybe a little old for playing games. Do you know what I'm trying to say?"

Now Maggie leaned forward, put both her hands on the table, palms down. "Yes," she said. "I know what you're trying to say, Connor. I'm not a kid." In her mind Maggie could hear Michelle all the way from Houston, saying, "That's it Maggie. Go for it." Maggie leaned closer, her voice now a whisper. "You're trying to say, 'Let's have sex.'"

Connor dropped his head to the table, then lifted it with a laugh. "Oh, God," he said. "From the very first, I said to myself, 'Now Connor, this Maggie woman, she's a straightforward, no-nonsense kind of gal.' And I'll be damned if I wasn't right."

"Straightforward? No nonsense?" Maggie's eyes lit up. "I guess so. I'd rather be like Susan Sarandon, sexy, giving off all sorts of sensual vibes. But I'm not. I'm straightforward, no-nonsense Maggie O'Neill. In high school all the boys thought I had a great personality."

"What I meant was . . ." Connor tried to interrupt, but Maggie shook her head.

"It's all right, Connor. You'd like to go to bed with me, and, honestly, I'd like that, too. But not only am I straightforward and no-nonsense with a great personality, I'm a little old-fashioned, I guess. Old-fashioned enough to want a little romance, at least something more than 'I like you,' from a man who's a little lonely, a little horny, and a little drunk. Maybe some other time." Maggie stood up.

She heard Michelle groan. "You blew it, girlfriend," Michelle said. "Practically had him between the sheets and told him adios."

"I know it, Michelle," Maggie snapped back under her breath.

Maggie fumbled through her purse. "I need my Blazer key."

"The drinks are on me." He slid the key across the table.

"I'm sorry. I'm really beat. A long, long day and everything just seems so difficult. It's really not you. Just bad timing."

Connor shrugged. "Forget it. Caca happens, as they say down here in old Mexico. I am lonely," he said, "and horny. More than a little. But I'm not drunk. I know what I said. 'I like you' isn't bad. A hell of a lot better in my book than telling someone you hardly know 'I love you' and not meaning it." He shook his head and sighed. "I guess we're in two different places. I can accept that. Yeah," he said, "maybe some other time."

Later, Connor wandered the streets for an hour or so, searched out places he hadn't been, moving south from the zócalo past the Benito Juárez market, easing across the streets that now were thinning as shopkeepers clanged down their metal doors for the night.

What a strange and disturbing day. Connor really did admire Maggie and found her appealing on many levels. Then why had he sabotaged what seemed to be a blossoming relationship? Or maybe it wasn't him at all. Had Maggie overreacted? Was this something she couldn't help after those years of caring for and resenting her mother? Still some bottled-up anger?

Connor stopped outside a mezcal bar. He peered over the swinging doors, breathed in the smoke of cigarettes and the faint sweetness of the mezcal. For a moment he soaked up the laughter and the talk, the gleam of bottles behind the bar, and felt the pull of easy mindlessness followed by easy answers that would repair things for tonight. But instead, he moved on down the street where he stopped for a moment and stared at some handmade, elaborately tooled boots in a shop window.

Then he caught his reflection in the glass, glimpsed something he had never seen before, something that disturbed him. He backed off a couple of steps, and a truck gave him two quick honks and roared on by. Connor wanted to see the full length of his image in the glass, wanted to get the whole picture to better comprehend what had caught his eye, but he couldn't without backing into the street. He looked both ways, a taxi in one direction, but it was a couple of blocks away. He started to step back again, but didn't, afraid that in Mexico at night it would be foolish to take the risk, even to see things more clearly.

CHAPTER 13

Ginger wandered through Señora Velez's gallery and eased out
into the open courtyard behind. She stopped and glanced back. Señora
Velez had cornered a couple of gringa shoppers next to a stack of fabric
purses. With a glance, Ginger checked the watercolor studio and spotted
someone there, probably Connor; she hoped he wouldn't spot her.

He was good with his medium, she had to admit that, but he had a way
of watching her, his disarming way of making small talk, and a sort of surface
innocence that had its charm. But she sensed it was all part of an act.

She had seen it before, the way some men, mostly tenured professors,
had of moving along the edge of an undefined boundary. The skillful ones
used their friendliness and a sense of humor to keep themselves from whatever lay on the other side. Lay was the right word, Ginger knew, and didn't
want to go close to that with Connor.

She lingered in the courtyard for a few minutes, stopping by the pond
where koi nibbled at the stems of calla lilies. She waited with one eye on the
studio, hoping that Connor wouldn't suddenly appear, hoping instead to
spot Rafael. She glanced up. The door to his upstairs room was shut, and he
wouldn't be there, she knew, not after five. He could be in the back room of
the gallery, for the side door was open, but Ginger didn't dare go there.

Andean flute music, the same repetitive stuff that Señora Velez was for-ever playing, drifted from the gallery. Through the back window she spotted a fresh gaggle of tourists, talking and pointing. They could be talking to Rafael, but Ginger didn't want to see him there, with Señora Velez around.

The sky had turned a deep violet. By seven, it would be dark. She moved to a corner of the courtyard and found a bench where she had a view of the gallery, bright with light and bold with weavings and, already, Day of the Dead skeletons.

Oh, Ginger, she thought, how did you get yourself into this, anyway? She felt as if she were sixteen again. Only worse. With a sixteen-year-old's excitement and a thirty-eight-year-old woman's mind and history. What am I doing, she thought, and suddenly caught a glimpse of who and where she was: a competent artist, one of an MFA breed that seemingly overpopu-lated the world, a not-so-young female traveling alone in a strange country, a lonely woman, waiting to "accidentally" cross paths with a younger man who had only a few weeks before become her lover. But it was all so tricky. Rafael worked or was out at the university almost all the time. And he was married. "God, this is crazy," she whispered.

Ginger casually glanced up at Rafael's closed door once more, then non-chalantly stood and looked around the courtyard again. In a moment she hurried back through the gallery and out to the street, then turned downhill toward the center of the city.

A slender man dressed in white watched as she moved down Alcalá, then followed, always staying no more than a half a block behind. But Ginger never noticed him and would not have known Leonardo, Rafael's brother-in-law, even if she had seen him.

To get to the zócalo from the gallery on Alcalá you cross Independicia, a main thoroughfare through the middle of Oaxaca, and then on to a plaza that has as its focal point the cathedral. The alameda is completely paved with squares of cut stone, so there are no paths, no walkways, and the scene there is one of seemingly random confusion.

The alameda at this hour of the early evening, with the time of siesta over, came alive with vendors. Some clutched the strings of dozens of helium-filled balloons that pulled upward; others set up tables with rows of silver jewelry or spread blankets thick with carved masks of goats and bulls and devils.

Women sat before piles of rebosos and embroidered dresses; men squatted next to stacks of woolen rugs from Teotitlan del Valle. Bacon-wrapped wieners, on the way to becoming Mexican hot dogs, sizzled on grills next to vats of steaming corn. The military band stormed the alameda with its brass music.

A cart filled with deep tins of ice cream held flavors that Ginger had never imagined: rose petal and prickly pear and *quemada*. Ginger had tasted them all. One of her problems, she knew, was not saying no to the foreign, the exotic. Some people harbor xenophobia; Ginger's weakness was the opposite, xenophilia. She loved it all.

She turned away from the crowds, from the noise, and meandered to the entrance to the cathedral, stopping just outside its carved wooden doors. Almost without thinking she passed an old woman begging, hand outstretched, and eyes milky. Ginger dug around in her fanny pack and dropped a few coins into her hand, then hurried inside to the cool darkness and quiet. Her eyes took a moment to adjust to the dim light, then she watched the shadows that danced on the wall behind scores of flickering candles.

She absorbed the strangeness of the cathedral, the faces chiseled into the columns and the saints that lined the walls. Ginger moved quietly down a side aisle and stopped at an altar. A draped Christ hung on a golden cross, not the happy, white-skinned Christ of the PTL club back home, but Christ with bloody punctures in his body. Christ suffering, with darkened skin and a tangle of black hair.

Behind the Christ figure a huge pyramid of silver milagros was stitched onto red velvet. Ginger moved on, the marble floor smooth and quiet beneath her sandaled feet, moving past a series of *nichos* that held the saints, until she settled into an ancient, smoke-stained pew.

The nichos. Ginger nodded to herself, remembering the first time she had noticed Rafael, had given him more than a glance, was near a nicho such as these. He was working in the courtyard behind the gallery, resurfacing a nicho for Señora Velez, smoothing out the old concrete surface before repainting it. Ginger had stopped and watched him work, the way he mixed the lime and cement and sand with water, stirring with his trowel, then lifting a trowel of the mixture and letting it plop back into the bucket, testing it, then adding a little more sand, stirring it again until it reached the perfect consistency.

Then Rafael drew a deep breath and took a mouthful of water from a cup, leaned close to the nicho and spewed the water out in a fine spray, evenly wetting the old surface so that the new concrete would stick. He did this three or four times, coating half of the surface. Then he wiped his mouth with his sleeve and with quick flips of his wrist tossed trowels of concrete on the old surface and began the smoothing process.

While he worked he glanced back at Ginger and spoke to her for the first time, and his good English startled her. His uncle was a stonemason who had taught him everything, how to work with mortar and concrete, how to patch old surfaces and make them look new, or the new look old. "An artesano," Rafael called his uncle.

Ginger listened and watched. To her Rafael looked as if he could have been at Monte Alban centuries before, laying stones for the structure that overlooked the ball court. When he stretched to reach the top of the nicho, his shirt pulled away from his jeans, and Ginger glimpsed the smoothness of his skin and felt an urge to reach out and run her fingers across the flatness of his taut belly. Her mouth went dry, and she turned and left without a word.

After that she and Rafael met at Del Jardín for drinks in the early evening, always with Connor and some of his students. But later they met alone, away from the zócalo at the cafe Santa Fe or upstairs in a dark corner at Primavera. They talked at first, a stream of words that rushed back and forth. Rafael seemed starved for words; he devoured them, her magical words about life in the States.

It was unsettling, but no grand surprise when Ginger and Rafael moved beyond casual chatter, beyond working on Ginger's Spanish pronunciation. They both had fallen silent. Ginger fiddled with an empty bottle of *agua mineral*, tilting it first one way and then the other, working it as if she were a smoker who no longer smoked. She had pulled her reboso off her shoulders and draped it across the back of her chair. She tried to cross her legs, but the table was too low. She slipped her feet from her sandals and rubbed the soles across the cool tiles of the floor.

Then, without thinking, she lightly touched Rafael's arm in a way that even that first time seemed to be natural, more a reflex than flirtation.

Rafael leaned toward her then and touched her one silver earring, a miniature skeleton that dangled from her ear, and let his hand slide slowly down her neck. It was all over then. The game had changed, Ginger knew. A surreptitious kiss when Rafael left first, and a quick squeeze of his hand held an unnamed promise.

Now Ginger moved through the cathedral and stopped once more, this time before the Virgen de la Concepcion. "Oh, please," she whispered, "forgive this poor woman for she knows not what the hell she does." Ginger waited quietly. She watched the other women who on that late afternoon had come and knelt and lit candles and prayed: those dressed in the black of their mourning, those bent and crippled and frail, those young and proud and struggling with temptation. All for their own reasons desiring deliverance from the pain of their lives.

From the back of the cathedral, Leonardo, the slender man in white, held his hat in his hand and watched her every move.

When Ginger emerged from the darkness of the cathedral onto the alameda, she looked up. There at the top of a pole a huge Mexican flag hung limply above her. She stared up for a moment, tried to envision the flag in a painting some way, maybe fractured or tilted with the cathedral in the background, with some irony involved.

A stupid idea, she thought, knowing her heart wasn't in creating new paintings, not today. From out of nowhere the military band started up the national anthem. While Ginger watched, a group of sturdy Oaxacan policemen lowered the flag and carefully folded it into a bulky triangle. As one unit the band and the policemen all marched off in unison. Ginger fell in behind them as they moved away. Without thinking, she marched along, left, right, left, right. She almost sang to the rhythm of the march, feeling that this gave her purpose, this not wandering, not knowing where she was headed, just with someone to lead the way.

When the flag brigade passed Del Jardín Ginger stepped off to the side. The tables under the portal were almost all full, and she scanned the restaurant for someone she knew, for a table she could share with anyone, just so she wouldn't have to be alone. But she saw only strangers. She would wait.

Connor would be along later for his shot of mezcal and a beer, and in all likelihood Maggie would be with him, for after keeping her distance from them all the last few days, Maggie had once again joined the after-class gatherings. And maybe Rafael would show up, too. If Señora Velez didn't keep him late he always tagged along with Connor.

The two men had become pals, it seemed, drinking their coffee and chocolate together early most mornings—Rafael had told her that; he listened to Connor's bullshit and believed most of it, evidently. And worst of all Rafael thought Connor was a great artist, and now he was taking drawing lessons from him. Why does everyone think they can be an artist? Why does Connor lead Rafael along when he should be studying for his university course? Connor must be after something.

Connor is a fake, Ginger figured. Just because he can render a landscape with a little flair. Variations on an old, old theme. Tired and exhausted. Art for traditional colleges and little old ladies. In truth, not real art at all.

Ginger could paint that way, too, with oils. That's what she did in Colorado —mountain scenes, aspen trees fluttering yellow in the wind. And here in Mexico, the prints she pulled with the Virgin of Guadalupe crap. She had talent, but, also, could deliver what would sell.

Ginger felt herself become agitated. She tried to remember her prayer in church. For serenity? Or acceptance? Maybe all she needed was awareness. She took a deep breath. "I need to get back to my yoga," she whispered. She found a vacant table and quickly ordered a margarita, no salt. Okay, Ginger, she thought. You're in Oaxaca; just relax, enjoy yourself. Go to Monte Alban, go to Mitla, take a crash course in Spanish, be productive, for God's sake. Forget about Rafael. You know how that will end up anyway—crash and burn, one way or the other. Forget about Connor; he'll just mess with your mind, get you off the track. You don't need any man.

But in spite of herself Ginger looked up the street, hoping to spot Rafael and Maggie and Connor coming her way. But, no, nothing but strangers.

She turned back toward the action on the zócalo. A man dressed in white caught her eye, the way he stared at her from where he stood under one of the giant laurel of India trees. Ginger turned away. She was used to men staring. Not that she was young anymore, but still attractive, and knew she possessed a magnetism when she entered a room. But men here in Mexico stared anyway, because they were Latinos, she thought, and it is their cultural duty to flirt and stare.

A young Mexican strolled by with his guitar and gave Ginger a little bow. He strummed a chord and asked if she would like to hear a special song, maybe a love song.

Ginger shook her head. No, gracias, she told him. He nodded, strummed the same chord, and started to step away. He spotted some change on the next table left for a waiter's tip. He strummed the guitar again and looked around. His eyes went from the coins on the table and back to Ginger. Finally, he eased to the edge of the table and with a quick movement raked them into his hand. He looked at Ginger once more and waited, as if to say, "You can do what you want. My fate is in your hands."

"Hey, I'm not exactly Miss Innocent, myself," she said, and didn't make a move. The guitarist gave her an almost imperceptible nod and a wink, and wandered away, strumming that same chord.

Just as Ginger pushed back her chair to leave she spotted Maggie and Connor winding their way toward her. Good, she thought, I'll stay and see what happens.

CHAPTER 14

The evening at Del Jardín turned out to be awkward at best. Connor acted agitated from the start for some reason, wanting to go somewhere else, somewhere new, a place around the corner he had heard about, a place where students wouldn't find him. "It's Saturday," he told Maggie, looking around the tables to see if any from his class were nearby. "And Señora Velez won't pay overtime." He glanced at Ginger and checked her drink, but the three of them stayed put.

Maggie tried to compensate for Connor's discontent, reminding herself all the while that this was Connor's problem, not hers. She asked Ginger about her work and after her second margarita Ginger made a series of crazy sketches on napkins to give Maggie some idea, but they were hardly more than random pen marks, and Ginger finally wadded the whole mess into a ball and stuffed it in her fanny pack.

A couple of students stopped by the table but didn't stay long. Eduardo blew smoke rings across at Connor, and Maggie could see Connor get antsy. She didn't know if he would leap across the table and strangle Eduardo or simply bolt and run. But in a few minutes Eduardo and his pal spotted some friends across the zócalo and left.

"Thank God," Connor muttered, and Maggie laughed. "I can't stand those young smart-ass guys," he said. "Oh to be rich and famous." He put his hand to his ear and turned toward the interior of Del Jardín. "A telephone call for me, you say. For me?"

"Excuse me ladies," he said, and pushed back from the table. "A call from New York. It must be my agent." Ginger laughed and watched Connor make his way to the back, headed to the men's room.

"A character," Ginger said, shaking her head. Then she turned to Maggie who, with a practiced waggle of her finger, was warding off a vendor. "Only twenty pesos," the boy crowding the table said. He held up some thin silver bracelets. "Puro," he said. "For you, fifteen pesos." But Maggie shook her head and turned away, and he wandered off.

"You and Connor," Ginger said, and pushed her margarita glass to one side. She leaned forward. "Do you have something going on?"

Maggie smiled and felt herself blush. "We're friends," Maggie said. "Off and on, but friends."

Ginger watched Maggie, the way her eyes lit up when she talked. Somehow she managed to be serious and in control, but still awake to the unknown possibilities of her life. Ginger wished she could be more like that, and thought she would have matured past her impulsiveness and quick temper and become more at ease by now.

"Just friends," Maggie repeated. "No more or less. At least for now. Connor's not the easiest man in the world to read. Or to get close to."

"I don't really know him," Ginger said. "I couldn't really say, but he seems like an okay guy."

"The good, the bad," Maggie said. "And some days, the bad and the good. Hard to figure out." Then she got quiet, staring off into the trees across the way. "I'm still trying to figure him out. I hope I've learned by now to be cautious. I've been on my own, you know, only a couple of months."

"I want to see your photographs sometime," Ginger said, hoping to ease the tension she felt.

Suddenly Ginger sensed someone at her shoulder, but didn't turn. A woman conditions herself not to turn, especially in Mexico. But she saw Maggie's face light up and at the same time heard Rafael's precise voice behind her asking, "Where is the professor?"

Rafael borrowed a chair from the next table and slid it close to Ginger. When he sat down he squeezed her hand under the table.

Later, as the evening and the margaritas went on, as the talk and the joking and laughing slowed down, Ginger found herself standing at the bar inside Del Jardín with Rafael. While the bartender looked on and interjected his own personal tips, Rafael demonstrated the salt and lime and shots of tequila technique that Ginger never had figured out. She had passed her limit, so faked her way through the motions.

She stared back through the front of the cafe, out toward the street where Connor now leaned close to Maggie. With elaborate gestures he seemed to be intently explaining something that appeared to be, from his expression, his own theory of the evolution of the human species.

Ginger found a pen within reach down the bar, and on a napkin, while Rafael and the bartender argued and bantered, she wrote, "30 minutes. La Mansion, room 16." Ginger folded the napkin, took Rafael's hand and folded it around the napkin. She left without looking back.

Outside, Ginger stopped to let Maggie and Connor know she was going to El Toro, a cafe around the corner, and that Rafael would join her in a few minutes. "He loves their *tasajo*," she explained. "See you tomorrow," she said, touching Maggie's shoulder, then hurried away without looking back, not giving them a chance to say they would join them.

On Independencia she turned left, moving quickly past shopkeepers sliding their metal doors down with a clank, locking them until morning. Then north on Porfirio, facing the last charging buses that braked coming down the steep hill.

Finally, at the top of a rise, Ginger hurried across the street to her hotel, through the carved wooden doors and past the night clerk, who nodded without taking his eyes off the glow of a television behind the desk. She dug into her purse for her key, stumbling a little as she went.

Ginger had stayed at the Hotel Principal for her first days in Oaxaca, but soon discovered La Mansion, this small hotel hidden from the street by high walls, and she had been there ever since. La Mansion was no mansion at all, but only a five-minute walk to the alameda or to the gallery on Alcalá, and cost half as much as Hotel Principal. The rooms surrounded a courtyard choked with bougainvillea and roses and blossoming lime trees. She considered this her own secret garden.

She rose early most days and wandered the grounds, exploring until eight, when breakfast was served. The cook, a woman who always wore a blue-checkered apron and a white scarf, gathered *yerba santa* for her tamales and black beans, and other strange herbs for her chicken soup.

Ginger's room was small, but had a passable bed, a pine table that she used for her workspace, one straight-backed chair and a straw-seated, armless rocking chair. Now, after more than a month here, Ginger had claimed the room as her own. On the wall above the desk she had hung milagros and silver hearts and a Virgin of Guadalupe calendar. A vase held dried roses, and on a bedside table she had arranged three tin candleholders, each with a different colored candle. One of her multicolored paintings brightened another wall.

Now in the shadowed darkness of her room Ginger lit the three candles, then she lay across the bed and waited, listening for Rafael to knock.

CHAPTER 15

Sunday morning, All Saints' Day, and in Coyotepec a day of celebration especially in honor of Santiago, the patron saint of the local church. At least that's what Connor thought. He had a hard time keeping all the saints straight. But he knew this was Sunday, and knew he was headed to Coyotepec with Rafael, who had the day off from the gallery, and invited him a week ago.

Coyotepec was Rafael's village, the place where he lived when he wasn't staying in Oaxaca at the gallery, and an annual grand fiesta was happening today. "There will be food and mezcal and cerveza." Rafael told him. "And you can meet my family, all of them; Claudia, my wife, and Carlos, my son. Three of my brothers will be there, and my two sisters and my father and my mother and all of my cousins." Connor felt overwhelmed by the numbers of Rafael's relatives, but he was curious to see the village that was his young friend's home.

So now on this bright morning Rafael led the way as the two men moved along the streets of Oaxaca, headed for the *mercado de abastos* where they would catch a third-class bus that would carry them fifteen kilometers or so to Coyotepec. Connor toted a canvas bag slung over his shoulder. It held a small 35mm camera for snapshots, a pad of drawing paper, and a box of *caran d'arche* colored pencils. If things didn't work out Connor could always retreat from the celebration and sketch.

"You're certain that it's okay for me to come along?" Connor asked. "With your family, with the rest of the village?" Connor hurried the questions between breaths as he pushed hard to keep pace with Rafael.

Rafael glanced back. "Of course," he said. "You are my guest. There is no problem."

Earlier Connor had eased out of bed with a dull headache that he couldn't shake, and now had second thoughts about the whole thing. It had sounded like a small diversion when Rafael asked him the week before, but Connor hadn't counted on a night like Friday. Not just a little too much of the drink, but too many hours sitting late at Del Jardín. And now he felt like hell. His surefire cure of a banana, papaya, and yogurt smoothie hadn't fazed his hangover at all.

Connor stopped for a moment in the shade of a building. He took off his hat, the straw he had picked up when he had an adventure of a different sort with Maggie. All the campesinos wore these hats, but now he wondered why. The weave was tight with no vent holes. The heat trapped around his head, which felt as if it would explode. He wiped his face with his shirtsleeve and took a deep breath, trying to slow his breath. The stench from an open drain next to the street rose up around him. Connor had an iron-clad stomach and never threw up, but this morning he wasn't so sure.

"You are okay?" Rafael had stopped ahead of him, waiting. "You want to catch a taxi now?"

"I'll be okay. Just give me a minute." He shifted the canvas bag to his other shoulder. "I just have something in my shoe." He leaned against a wall and lifted one foot up and tugged at his sock and said, "That's better. Let's go."

As they moved on Connor watched Rafael, marveled at how easily he moved through the now-crowded streets. Connor felt a vague sense of regret, but refused to stay there.

As they neared the mercado Rafael picked up his pace. Connor struggled after him, dodging men who pushed carts heavy with mangoes and papayas and black or green pottery; one overloaded with huge baskets filled with blue speckled pots and pans. He stepped around vendors who squatted in front of plastic sheets lined with rows of candies that swarmed with bees.

Connor wondered how late Rafael had been the night before. How could he stay up most of the night, wake early enough to clean up the gallery's mess from the night before, and now appear fresh and eager, full of energy? I could have, Connor thought, at one time. And by God I still could, for the right reasons. Or maybe for the right person.

He thought of Ginger again, her quickness to laugh and her quickness to snap back in anger. She would be a handful. Then he thought of Maggie and her drive and her talent. That's more your speed, old fellow, a realization that brought him a surprising sense of relief.

Coyotepec turned out to be much larger than he thought, and was laid out almost like a smaller version of Oaxaca; a central plaza with shops and restaurants on all sides. The sprawl of a giant ceiba tree at the edge of the plaza provided shade from the intense sun. A scattering of houses thinned out away from town.

They stopped at the pristine parish church, which had been built in the sixteenth century. Rafael turned and looked back. "From here you can see my family's house, there," he pointed. "The yellow house with the metal roof."

"The one with the field next to it? And the big dead tree?" It was less than a kilometer away, an easy walk. "A field, yes," Rafael said, "enough for a garden and a place for my father's goats."

Connor and Rafael moved close to the massive wooden front doors where Connor could hear the distinctive monotone drone of a priest conducting some ceremony of the church inside.

"He's not our real priest," Rafael said, gazing up at the image of Bartholomew the Apostle above the doors. "Our real priest, he still lives here, in the town, in the parish house that we, the people of Coyotepec own, with the woman he loves. The church won't let him serve us, said he must go, but he stays in town because he has been the priest for more than twenty years." He shrugged. "This new one, he doesn't even live here, just comes when we must have a priest. But no one likes him. He brought too many of the old church's ways with him. A stupid, hardheaded priest." Rafael spit to one side. "Even my mother doesn't like him."

"Must be hard for you all," Connor said, although the mysterious workings of the Catholic Church held no interest for him. But he could understand the lure of a woman versus celibacy.

Out to the side of the church a low rock wall surrounded the cemetery where Connor could make out worn-down mounds with tilted wooden crosses and newer, more elaborate headstones and ornate plaques. Rafael gazed out across the cemetery for a few moments, and Connor figured it was filled with generations of his ancestors.

Across the way a woman peddled bouquets of bone-colored lilies. Scores of Coyotepec's famous black pots filled a rug on the ground next to her. A man scooped ice cream from a metal can strapped to his chest. Then around the side of the church a small procession made its way past them, and Rafael waved. Two women carried a platform covered with creamy satin that held the figurine of a saint. A couple of old men and some children tagged along behind. In a moment the entire contingent disappeared into a side door of the church.

"One of them is my aunt, my mother's sister," Rafael said. "They are getting ready for this afternoon." Then he turned and pointed out into a bare field where men were placing empty beer bottles in a circle. "It will be a grand fiesta," Rafael said. "Fireworks. Rockets tonight."

Rafael looked back at the church. "This is where Claudia and I were married. More than four years ago." He got quiet for a moment. "I like to come here when it is quiet. It is a place I go when I have to be alone. When I need to—how do you say—make my plans."

"When you have problems," Connor said. "Do you have problems now?"

Rafael shrugged, but didn't answer. Connor watched Rafael a minute, then without thinking, he asked the question that had been eating at him for weeks. "You and Ginger," he said. "There's something going on with you?"

He shook his head. "We are friends," he said, his voice even and low. "Ginger is a nice woman. She likes me, likes to practice speaking my language. We are friends. That is all."

A nice speech, Connor thought. Well rehearsed, it seemed, as if Rafael had anticipated this question, from him or someone else.

"Whatever you say," Connor finally said. "But where were you last night, my friend? When you and Ginger went over to El Toro, you said you would come back. Maggie and I waited for you. She finally gave up and left and I stayed. Shut the damned zócalo down. You and Ginger never showed." Connor stopped and waited for Rafael to say something, but the young man simply stared out over the distant hills as if he wished he were there.

"Anyway," Connor went on, "you need to know how it appears. To me, to Maggie, you two seem to be more than friends."

Rafael turned. He shook his head and pointed his finger at Connor. "If you were a young man, like me, then you would understand."

"Hey, I'm not that old," Connor said. "But I have had more experience with women, especially with gringas. And I'm not trying to interfere, but I just . . ."

"You just want Ginger for yourself." Rafael spit to one side. "I have seen the way you watch her. I know the way you look at her. But she likes me. She is my friend. How can I help that? Is that my fault?"

"Hey, don't get so hot," Connor said, and put his hand on Rafael's shoulder. "Forget it. It's just that you have a young wife and a son, and I wanted to keep you out of trouble, if I could."

"Maybe yes, maybe no," Rafael said. He pulled away, and before Connor could answer, Rafael took off down the hill from the church, headed for the school. In a minute he stopped, turned, and gave Connor a grin. "Come on, my friend," Rafael said. "This is the day of our fiesta. You worry too much about everything." Rafael laughed. "We will—how do you say—make a deal. You worry about Profesor Connor and I will worry about Rafael."

Connor grinned with relief. "Okay, okay," he said. Now he was sorry he had ever brought Ginger up to Rafael. It wasn't any of his business, Connor knew. And he knew, also, that his motivations might not be so pure, that maybe he did want more than to keep Rafael out of trouble with his wife.

Rafael waited while Connor followed the path down to where he stood. "Just one more damned thing, though." He moved closer to Rafael, his voice low and threatening, his finger almost punching the young man's chest.

Rafael pulled back and clenched his fist.

"Where in the hell is this fiesta, anyway?" Connor asked. "And where in the hell is the cerveza?" Rafael laughed and gave Connor a high five and the two men hurried down the hill.

They stopped at the basketball court by the school and watched a hot four-on-four half-court game. After a goal, one of the boys tossed the ball to Rafael, and they talked while Rafael bounced the ball easily without looking. Connor could tell, mostly from their gestures and the movement of their eyes, that some of the talk was about him, but it all went too fast to catch.

He and Rafael moved on then, Connor waving a friendly adios to the boys, Rafael grinning back at them as they started up the game once more.

"They wanted us to play," Rafael said. "But I told them I had to see my family first." He turned to Connor and grinned, then moved on down the path walking backwards, still facing Connor, still grinning. "And I told them you were too old to play."

"One on one," Connor said. "You just wait. I'll take you on and I'll teach you a thing or two. You'll see who's too old." Rafael laughed and trotted on down the path, leading the way to his father's house.

There was cerveza, the bottles drawn up in a perforated bucket from the cool water of a well. The bottles were passed to the men first, and then to the women. Most of the men sat on benches or squatted on their haunches under the skeletal remains of a dead eucalyptus tree. A couple of the men held guitars by the necks while they drank, and others rested brass horns across their laps.

Out behind the house boys kicked around a worn-smooth soccer ball, while some other kids dug a tunnel into the side of a small gravel hill.

Connor stood next to Joaquin, Rafael's father, and both were quiet while they sipped their beers. He had felt awkward when Rafael left them after a brief introduction, moving quickly to the house to find Claudia and Carlos. Joaquin spoke hardly any Spanish, but carried on a one-way conversation with Connor anyway, in a mix of Spanish and Mixtec. Connor hardly understood a word the older man said, but every so often he nodded his head and said, "*Claro*," or "*Comprendo*."

Rafael's mother soon joined them and interrupted every second or third sentence to correct her husband. Joaquin never looked her way, just raised his voice to repeat what he had said more emphatically. The universal language of marriages, Connor figured.

One by one, Rafael's brothers wandered by. Connor studied their faces, noted the roughness of their hands when he shook them, their awkwardness when they stood next to him. They seem much older than Rafael, but possessed none of his sureness. It was as if they belonged only there in the town. That some ancestral line had been drawn, a long string of life that had in that place stretched back hundreds, maybe thousands of years.

Rafael seemed different. Not of his family and not of this small town. He had broken that string, it seemed.

The house was nicer than Connor expected, and new, its walls rough-finished concrete. Through the open door he spotted smooth concrete floors. Nothing fancy about it at all, purely functional, but there were nice touches here and there. Barro negro pots, some cracked, were filled with leggy geraniums and lined the front walkway and were crowded under the overhang of the front porch. A small nicho to the left of the front door held a plaster version of some saint. The shrine was thick with the black of burned candles.

Connor moved away from Joaquin and wandered around the yard to the side of the house. There, outside, he found the kitchen, which joined the house all along one side, tucked back under an overhang where coals from a small fire in a circle of rocks gave off a faint glow.

In this outdoor kitchen several women worked around a long pine table, patting and mixing and rolling dough, for tamales or tortillas, Connor hoped. A couple of them were obviously pregnant, and another had a reboso-wrapped baby strapped to her breast so that her arms were free. No infertility problem here, Connor thought.

While the women talked and worked they cut their eyes back and forth at Connor, then covered their mouths and laughed quietly. Connor felt uncomfortable, as if some joke was going around the table, and the joke was about him.

Farther on he discovered a kiln with black shards strewn on the ground in front and a few cracked pots stacked to one side, leaning on the stone structure. He heard someone coming his way and turned to see Joaquin hobbling along, almost dragging his left leg behind him. Rafael hadn't told him that his father was crippled. Okay, Connor thought, no wonder the boy works so hard, is driven.

Joaquin pointed to a goat out to one side, standing on a trash pile, and began going on about the goat in Spanish that Connor could mostly make out. He was by now about as comfortable with Spanish as Joaquin must be. Connor gathered that Joaquin had bought this goat three years back for a good price at the Zaachila market, and Joaquin had some hard times after that. He frowned and pointed at his lame leg.

But he kept the goat, didn't sell it for the money he needed. And now, he said, as he waved his arm out towards the valley, look at this.

Connor turned and saw a couple of small boys moving a herd of goats up the hill. There were a dozen or so goats of all colors and sizes.

Joaquin beamed. "Money is no good," he said, and spit on the ground between his boots. "You have pesos in your hand and then, poof, they are gone," and he gestured toward the sky. "Like a cloud they disappear."

"But this goat, my neighbors borrow him for their ewes, and in a while there are goats everywhere. They give me one sometimes, if there are two, or they will bring me some alfalfa or whatever they grow." He nodded with satisfaction. "There is nothing else I need."

He turned to hobble away, then turned back. "Buy a goat," he said. "Whatever happens do not sell it, and you will never be poor."

"The only better thing is to have sons, and I have four of them." He held up his open hand for Connor see, and nodded his head as if to affirm something sacred. Then he wobbled slowly away.

Connor wondered what Maggie would say to this. The wisdom of fathers, he thought, with a shake of his head. We all live with the curse of our fathers' wisdom. His own father had given him advice and repeated it over the years until he died seven years ago: "Get a good job and don't lose it. Go to church every Sunday. Support your family." Connor didn't care to be measured by his father's wisdom, and Rafael, he guessed, would never own a goat. So much for fatherly advice.

Connor moved on around the house and was about to go back over and join Joaquin under the tree to have one more beer. But just at that moment Rafael appeared on the porch, followed reluctantly, it seemed, by Claudia. To Connor, Rafael's smile seemed forced and his sureness had vanished. A little boy scooted between them, headed for the other children who played at the edge of the field. Rafael grabbed at him and missed. "Carlos!" he yelled, but the boy didn't slow. Rafael muttered something that Connor figured was a curse and glared at Claudia as if to say, "Can't you control your son?"

Claudia backed away. She waited at the door a moment, dressed in her jeans and a faded, tie-dyed T-shirt that looked to Connor as if it had come out of the sixties. Her hair wasn't up in braids and ribbons like the other women's, but hung straight and soft, almost to her shoulders. The scar at the corner of her mouth gave her the same perpetual smile that he remembered from that night in Oaxaca when he first saw her. But her eyes sent a different message.

Claudia folded her arms over her breasts. She glared at Rafael, then turned and rolled her eyes at a group of the women who stared. Her mother-in-law gave her an impatient look and sighed, then whispered something to the women around her.

Connor remembered the way Claudia had danced with the santo during the fiesta at her father's house. She had seemed so much more at home, there in Oaxaca, that night a few weeks back, but here looked out of place.

Connor could see why Rafael and Claudia had found each other, neither one being content, it seemed, to live marginally in this small town the way Rafael's parents did. Both of them wanted out, he guessed, Rafael staying around the gallery and university more than was necessary, and Claudia probably going into Oaxaca to be with her family there whenever she could. Or maybe she didn't. Rafael might not like that for more than one reason.

These two were different from the others and couldn't help it, and in a moment anyone could sense the difference from the way they looked and dressed, more middle-class Oaxacan than traditional Mixtec or Zapotec.

Connor could only guess at the problems this created, and he felt a sadness come over him. God, what a long way they have to go, he thought. From here in Coyotepec, living in the back room of this house, and Claudia especially, going through the motions of their lives, and both having unfulfilled dreams. Dreams they had picked up from school or the false glitter of television, or from Rafael bringing back stories of tourists who wandered into the gallery.

Or dreams Rafael picked up from some visiting artist. Connor shook his head. Uh-uh, he thought, I don't want to be any part of this. For Connor had been through it all, the dreams and the disillusionments, and he wouldn't wish that trip on anyone.

Rafael motioned to Claudia, and they moved out into the sun. When she saw Connor she nodded, then whispered something to Rafael. Connor moved toward them.

Rafael looked from Claudia to Connor. "You have already met?" he asked Connor.

"Not exactly met," Connor said. "But, yes, I saw her one night in Oaxaca. At her father's house, I think. Her brother, Leonardo, asked me. There was a fiesta, a celebration, of some sort."

Connor shrugged. He had seen Rafael there, too, outside the gate, yelling at Leonardo, angry with Claudia, but he hardly knew Rafael then.

Rafael looked agitated. "Leonardo," he said, almost spat the name out. "Why didn't you tell me?" he asked, and Connor didn't know if the question was for him or Claudia.

Just then the band started up, a raucous tune, and Joaquin came limping from the house carrying two canning jars of what Connor took to be mezcal. Joaquin offered one to Connor, and he shook his head, held up his hand to refuse. But Joaquin insisted and Connor took it with a nod of thanks.

At that moment the music fell and then rose again to an energetic pitch. Connor held the jar of mezcal high. "Salud," he said to Joaquin, and took a sip. He raised the jar toward the band and took another sip, and the heat flowed all the way down. There would be no turning back now.

He held the mezcal out to Rafael. "And salud to you both. And much happiness." But Claudia turned away and slipped back into the shadows of the house, with Rafael only a couple of steps behind.

Later, after feasting on a half-dozen tamales, Connor sat on a low rock wall and watched the sky turn dark purple. Maybe it was only this time of year, but when the sun finally dropped, the clear sky of early night took on an inkiness that he had never encountered before, anywhere else.

He studied a bunch of slender, leafy twigs he held in his hand, a gift from Joaquin when the mezcal and beer were passed around for the last time. "*Polello*," he had called the herb, and the old man sniffed the leaves. "Drink all the mezcal you want," he said, "and with this you will never be drunk." Now Connor took a big sniff, hoping for the best.

The fiesta was done, it seemed, and the men had drifted off across the way to make plans for the next fiesta, Connor guessed, probably filtering more mezcal.

The women had gone, too, balancing on their heads bundles of tamales wrapped in giant banana leaves, hurrying their children along in front of them. Now the moon hung pale against the sky, just a couple of days this side of full, and as the women moved on down the road they glowed in the chalky light.

Rafael and Claudia had not reappeared, and apparently no one gave that a thought. Their time alone, Connor figured, stuck in the back room of that little house, only a closed door between them and all their kin milling in and out, and fireworks booming and spewing, and the band blaring the same three tunes they knew over and over. And the kids yelling as they ran in and out and around the outside of the house. Then the burro braying and the turkeys fussing at a barking dog. If you're young and you're hot for each other it would work, Connor thought with a nod.

Connor took another deep sniff of the polello. He wasn't sure what it did; made him a little dizzy, light-headed, maybe. Oh, well. When in Coyotepec . . .

Rafael suddenly appeared beside him. "We must go. Catch the last bus to town." Connor nodded, studied his face in the dim light of the moon, trying to read what might have happened between Rafael and Claudia the past couple of hours. He could envision the inevitable argument, the accusations, and the making up, and what always followed.

Then an argument once again as Rafael gathered up his things, getting ready to leave for another week.

"Are you ready? Are you okay? We'd better go," he said again. Connor nodded, and eased off the rock wall, stiff from sitting so long. He offered the polello to Rafael, but he just laughed and Connor tossed the bundle to the ground. "Maybe a Budweiser, later," he said. "Or a whisky, a Chivas Regal. If you will buy."

"Champagne taste, almost," Connor said. "The Americanos have taught you well." Champagne taste in women, too—Claudia, a lovely woman, with something special to give her a nice edge. And Ginger? More than a little there to interest any man.

Connor wondered if Rafael would see Ginger tonight when they got back, and if so, would she know if he had been with Claudia most of the afternoon? Or would she care?

The two men made their way back up the hill toward town. They stopped for a minute at the basketball court. A couple of boys still shot goals by the light of the moon. "One on one?" Rafael asked. Connor laughed and pointed toward the road. "Another time," he said. "I'd be way too tough for you in the dark."

CHAPTER 16

Monday morning, November 2. On the surface pretty much business as usual for Connor. He showered early, quickly before the hot water ran out, then brewed his little pour-through pot of coffee just as he did every other morning. Pan dulces from La Luna sat in a white paper sack on top of his refrigerator, the sack crumpled from Connor carting it around with him most of the night before. He was afraid the sweet rolls would be mostly crumbs by now. He would check them later, eat the pieces with a soup spoon if he had to.

This was official Day of the Dead in Mexico, and for Connor a special day of another sort. Today, Señora Velez would hang the group show with Rafael's help. Señora Velez had all of the watercolors, and yesterday afternoon they were lined up, leaning against the gallery wall. The formal opening reception wouldn't be until Saturday night, but Connor knew Señora Velez would have the show up by ten this morning when the gallery opened. Lots of tourists would be wandering the streets on this special day, and the Señora, and Connor, wanted a shot at their pesos.

Connor had settled on eight strong watercolors, and three of them highlighted Day of the Dead elements—loaves of the special bread, a profusion of marigolds, and even a skeleton or two.

Ginger had seen them and nodded her head in approval, but hadn't commented. He guessed what she was thinking, could almost see the words in cartoon bubbles above her head—commercial and opportunistic and appropriated. Hell, yes, he thought. As long as they sell, he didn't give a damn.

Connor stepped out on the balcony, coffee cup in hand. It was six-thirty, the air still cool, the first sunlight now refracting off the dew that covered the tile walkway below.

Across the way Rafael's door was half-open, an invitation as far as Connor was concerned, so he made his way around the open balcony. He moved slowly, cleared his throat a couple of times, then stopped and scraped the bottom of his boot on the cracked base of a concrete planter. Connor wanted Rafael to hear him coming, sort of an unspoken protocol between the two of them.

He whistled then as he moved again, a little off-key, and hummed the lyrics of some half-remembered song. Maggie would know those lyrics, he thought. He wanted to talk to her again, make certain that their earlier blow-up at Del Jardín was behind them.

Rafael stepped halfway through his doorway. "One minute, please. Would you like some chocolate?" Rafael was a hot chocolate man; he broke his morning bolillo in half and dipped it in his cup to soften it.

"No chocolate, thanks," Connor said, stopping outside Rafael's door. "I have my gringo coffee." The same exchange every morning.

Rafael stepped out on the balcony, carrying his mug. His white shirt was rumpled and his hair a little wilder than usual, still parted in the middle and thick and black, but bunched up in the back with a cowlick.

"A big day?" Connor said, feeling anxious about getting the show hung right. He was eager to get on with it, but Rafael seemed to be in no hurry, nodding as he sipped his chocolate.

"A big night?" Connor asked, his voice agitated.

Rafael shrugged. "Would you like a pan dulce?" Without waiting for Connor to answer, Rafael disappeared into his room and reappeared a moment late carrying a bakery sack.

They ate their rolls in silence, Connor not pursuing his question about last night, now sorry that he had asked. Rafael seemed content to stay silent, finishing off his roll.

"I'll meet you downstairs," Connor finally said. "See you in the gallery." He poured the last of his cold coffee over the balcony onto the grass below and made his way down the curved staircase into the back door of the gallery. He flipped on the overhead spots and surveyed the room. There were patch marks on the walls that had been touched up with slightly off-color splotches of paint, and one corner of the space didn't get much light, but the ceiling was high and the tall windows let in an abundance of natural light. Not bad, he thought. Lots of better galleries have worse spaces than this.

It would be a small show, all crowded into the back part of this large room, the rest of the gallery stuffed with standard Mexican stuff—carved animals from Arizola and pots from Coyotepec and rugs from Teotitlan del Valle. There were bunches of baskets and cases of silver jewelry, and in the front of the gallery an *ofrenda*, made especially for today, the Day of the Dead.

Hell, he thought, my watercolors will be lost in the middle of all this crap. Now he wished he had worked a little harder. Fourteen watercolors made an awfully small show, and only eight of them Connor's. Eight watercolors in eight weeks. Didn't sound too bad if you didn't know, he thought, but Connor could knock them out in a couple of hours each. What had he done for those eight weeks? He had taught three mornings a week to earn a few bucks. That was okay, but one painting a week for all those hours he had to work? A pretty pathetic output.

And now, when he saw them around the floor of the gallery, propped up against the wall, he knew he had fallen short, again. But these were bolder, a little more on the edge than his old work. Maybe Mexico with its contrasts of bright colors and *duende* had seeped into his subconscious and he hadn't even known it.

He moved on down the wall, inspecting his students' work, bending over just a little to check each painting. God, he thought, what can I do with Eduardo's? The young Mexican had painted a jungle scene from the Chiapas area, badly rendered vines and banana trees everywhere. In the foreground, in a ski mask, somehow looking as if he had just held up a convenience store, was subcommandante Marcos. He aimed his rifle at an unseen enemy. Too bad Marcos hadn't seen this watercolor and shot Eduardo! He moved the painting to the darkest corner of the gallery.

Maggie's painting turned out not bad at all. She had simply worked one of the standard still lifes from above, and by using that angle had distorted the shapes and forms in an interesting way, but technically a little stiff.

Ginger's piece was next, the paper she used larger than that of the other students, the fruit and vegetables from the still life brighter and bolder. It had a grotesque quality that mostly worked. Not pretty art, but not quite anti-art. "You'll see," Connor said to himself. "It won't sell. And nobody will give a damn if it is faux cutting edge." He straightened up and with a shrug, headed back to his room.

CHAPTER 17

That evening at Del Jardín Connor sat alone. From somewhere to the west another unseasonable rain had blown across the city, and then it cleared, showered again, and then cleared once more. Eduardo and Victor and a couple of their pals had wandered by early on, wet, and not seeming to care, not even looking Connor's way. Tourists were everywhere, dodging in under the portals that surrounded the zócalo, holding their cameras and guidebooks under their windbreakers, and then, when it cleared, stopping by the ofrendas that had been set up for this Day of the Dead.

The real ofrendas would be in the villages, where the processions to the cemeteries would take place later in the evening. Some tourists went there, trying to discreetly follow the locals. They seemed to want desperately to be participants in the ritual, or to capture on film something that could never be theirs.

Connor had no patience for that sort of thing. But he figured Maggie might go to some village where she had already been, and would be taking photographs most of the night. Let her go, Connor thought. He hoped all the tourists went and he could have the zócalo and Del Jardín to himself.

Connor was pleased now that the show had been hung. His watercolors came across strong, with a richness that surprised him. A little life left in this old dog, he thought. Don't count me out yet. Maybe he would get Maggie to take some slides of this new work and he would send them off to a gallery in Phoenix where he'd been in a group show before. Maybe they would grab these Mexican scenes.

Connor took a sip of tequila and chased it with a swallow of Dos Equis. Got to nurse this, he told himself. Maybe he would work on a couple of watercolors in the morning. A new start. He glanced around. Most of the other tables had filled while he was floating in his own world. Disco music boomed from the bar behind him, and out front a couple of fellows drummed each end of a long marimba like crazy.

Connor had tilted some chairs forward against the table to save a place for whoever might join him, but so far no one had showed up; with nowhere else to go, he would wait. In a few minutes he stood up and stretched, checking around before heading toward the bar with his eye on the Caballeros sign just past the television set near the back of the narrow room. The bartender saw him coming. He knew Connor from other days and other nights, and recognized the desperate look on his face, so poured a shot of Hornitos tequila and held it out. Connor laughed and shook his head. "No, amigo, but many thanks." He slid a couple of pesos across the bar and kept going. On his way back out he turned and watched the last round of a boxing match beamed out of Mexico City. A couple of featherweights danced around the ring with a whole lot of jabbing and feinting. They held their bright red gloves high in front of their faces while they bobbed and weaved, their satin boxing trunks pulled high, halfway to their armpits, as if they had made a pact of some kind to do no damage.

One of the boxers looked a lot like Rafael, enough to be his brother, and Connor hoped his young friend could avoid the blows of life as well as these boxers avoided being harmed.

The bell clanged the round to an end and Connor moved out toward his table. Rain had freshened the air and he took a deep breath. Day of the Dead, he thought. Here I am in Oaxaca, Mexico. Hard to believe.

Just after five Rafael showed up, ordered a Budweiser before he sat down, and in a couple of minutes, Ginger joined them. Connor had the feeling that she had been somewhere nearby, watching, but wouldn't show herself until Rafael came along.

"Nice watercolor," Connor said to Ginger. She nodded her thanks.

Rafael turned in his chair, asked a waiter for some peanuts, then said he would be right back.

Connor could tell that Rafael was uncomfortable. Well, let him squirm, Connor thought. You shouldn't get off completely free when you're married and screwing some other woman. Connor knew. He had paid in spades for screwing around. It serves Rafael right, dammit.

Ginger waited until Rafael had disappeared, then turned to Connor. "Which watercolor," she asked with a smile.

"You know," Connor said. Then added, "No games, please. The one in the gallery." Ginger shrugged.

"I guess you're aware of what you're doing," he said.

"Are you?" Ginger asked. "Aware of what you're doing? Are any of us?"

"Cut the philosophical bullshit," Connor said. "I just hate to see you screw up the kid's life. I mean his wife has to find out. They always do. And then what? You move on. And on. And then on some more. But it could be trouble for Rafael."

"It's none of your goddamned business, Connor. And he's no kid. I think you're just jealous. Rafael's young, he's alive, he's, well, he's something you never were, can never be."

"Shit," Connor hissed. "You're a real bitch, aren't you."

Rafael slid back into his chair. He looked at Ginger and then at Connor. He rolled his eyes to the sky and reached out his arms, as if he were trying to embrace the whole world. "I just love parties with my friends," he said. "Don't you?"

Rafael laughed then, and with a quick motion took Connor's hand in his, lifting it off the table. He nodded to Ginger and she hesitated, then put her hand on both the men's. "My good friends," he said, and Connor knew he meant it.

"Okay, okay," Connor said. "You damned diplomat." He looked at Ginger. "Sorry," he said. She nodded.

"I'm buying the drinks," Connor said. "This round, anyway." But he still burned inside, knowing that things weren't right, that somehow Ginger and Rafael always managed to stay one step ahead of him.

CHAPTER 18

By dusk the four of them—Maggie and Connor, Rafael and Ginger— had all settled in around a sidewalk table at Del Jardín. Connor was surprised when Maggie showed up, since she had been cool off and on, a little distant since their fiasco a couple of weeks ago. Neither of them had mentioned that evening, but even in the last class Connor had sensed her unease, even her distrust of him.

And this was Day of the Dead, for a photographer a time to be out hustling around the local cemeteries. Maggie always carried her camera, but settled it on the table now, the strap wrapped around one wrist, and ordered a margarita.

"Day of the Dead?" she said, when Connor wondered aloud why she was at Del Jardín on that special day. "It's okay, but photographers are everywhere. The next coffee table book you see will be of photographs of photographers taking Day of the Dead photographs."

Connor laughed. Maybe he and Maggie were over their rough spot. He hoped so.

"I realize that sounds awfully jaded," Maggie said, "And the ritual itself is quite touching, one with deep roots in this culture. But by now it's been done and done and done. That's just not my thing, anyway." And Connor nodded, knowing that.

"You saw the show?" Connor asked. "Rafael and I, with the Señora looking on, hung it this morning."

"I saw it," Maggie said. "I think I'll stick to photography." She laughed and patted her camera.

Maggie stared off across the zócalo. In a moment she lifted her camera to her eye and moved it slowly from right to left, then back again halfway and stopped.

At one time that would have annoyed him, a woman turning away from him for something or someone else, but since the day with Maggie in the village of Santa Maria del Rio, Connor watched Maggie with new-found respect. Then he turned back to his left where Ginger was bantering with Rafael.

"Jocks?" Ginger asked Rafael. "You know, jocks?" He grinned and shook his head. She turned to Connor. "Help," she said with a laugh.

"Jocks?" Connor said. "You know, fútbol players. Strong guys. Like this." Connor held his arms up and out, flexing his biceps, straining, as if to show off his muscles under his shirt.

Rafael nodded. "Athletes," he said and Ginger nodded. "Yes and no," she said. "A little different. Macho athletes. God, Connor, all I wanted to do is tell him that in the States Budweiser is a beer for jocks, but it's not that easy."

Connor pointed at the half-down bottle of Bud in front of Rafael, then drew a circle in the air with a slash across it. "No more Budweiser," he told Rafael. "It's bad for your image. You hang around with artists, you have to drink Scotch whisky or straight tequila or imported beer, for God's sake."

"Budweiser is imported," Ginger said, "here in Mexico," and she laughed again. She put her hand on Rafael's arm and rested her head against his shoulder.

Connor felt strangely embarrassed and looked away. Maggie leaned close to Connor. "They seem a little young?" she whispered.

Connor looked at Maggie in a quizzical sort of way. "Rafael, yes," he said. "Ginger?" He shrugged. Maggie pulled back. "Oh, you men!"

By dark the zócalo burst with movement under the glow of street lamps; skeletons of all sizes shook and ran and wobbled in the streets. Some puppets stood fifteen feet high with slits for eyeholes not far above their knees, while others were made from pasted colored paper. They danced before those who

128

sat around the tables at Del Jardín and circled around the benches and trees of the zócalo. They were made to scare and astonish and amuse—and some to be bought.

Then up on the bandstand the military band began trumpeting and drumming. Connor suddenly felt overcome by it all—the skeletons, the swarming crowds, the disco music from the bar and John Phillips Sousa across the way. Plus the boom of fireworks. Connor put both hands on the table to steady himself. Everything seemed to close in on him and he felt an urge to bolt.

He tapped Maggie's shoulder. "Let's go somewhere." She turned to face him. "I want to go somewhere and dance," he said. "Do you like to dance? Damn, but I wish Willie Nelson would show about now, not here, but somewhere quiet, with that beat-up old guitar. We could waltz across Texas for sure."

"Connor," Maggie said. "What in God's name has gotten in to you?"

He rested his hand on her shoulder, suddenly feeling sober, and she looked back, puzzled. "Let's get out of here," he said. "I don't want to dance, not really, but I need some quiet, something to eat." He rolled his eyes, nodded at Rafael and Ginger, still lost in each other. "I've been around too many years for all of this."

Maggie waited a minute and tried to read between his words, to see if there was something she needed to understand. But nothing seemed to be hidden. She nodded, put her camera over one shoulder and her canvas bag over the other. "You've paid?" she asked.

"I've paid and paid and paid," he said, rising from his chair.

CHAPTER 19

Maggie had felt trapped. A table of Europeans of unknowable origin crowded behind her, and on her left Rafael and Ginger were infatuated, oblivious to all else. The evening had moved beyond easy diversion and pleasure. Connor, disgruntled, seemed to want to be anywhere else but there, annoyed with Ginger, impatient with Rafael, or maybe just struggling with his own private demons. She had no way to know.

Now late into this Day of the Dead, Oaxaca's center suddenly lost its charm, the fireworks exploding threateningly close, and young boys tore through the streets waving three-foot long sparklers. The skeleton figures wandered, seemingly lost, as if they might vanish at the end of the evening, but came closer. Some of them rushed back and forth across the street, yelling and taunting. They had become aggressive, confronting the outlying tables of tourists, insisting on being photographed, then demanding pesos.

Maggie stayed determined not to let anything rattle her, and she boldly panned her camera across the way as if she had some particular scene she wanted to find, but more as a strategy to contain it all in some defined format. She should simply leave, but a vague inertia held her in place.

Her camera stopped for the third time on that same slender man dressed in white. He had been there for hours, it seemed, half-hidden behind one of the giant trees, always staring their way. Maggie felt hassled at being watched, and had had about enough.

"Connor," she said, touching his arm. "What is that character up to? The one over there, at the edge of the zócalo, watching us that way?"

Connor glanced around. "Who knows with this crazy crowd? Let's go somewhere else," he said. "I know, let's go somewhere where we can dance. Do you like to dance? Can you waltz?"

Maggie laughed.

"Anyway," he grinned. "I need some quiet, something decent to eat. What do you say?"

Maggie nodded. She felt the same way.

"Besides, I'm tired of all this." Maggie guessed by "this" he meant Rafael and Ginger. Or maybe the craziness all around.

Maggie reached for her purse, but Connor told her he'd already paid. "Paid and paid and paid."

Maggie laughed. "Well, you don't have to pay anymore."

Connor reached out and took Maggie's hand, grasped it firmly, as if he knew what he was up to, and she gave a little squeeze back.

Connor reached over to Rafael, put a hand on the young man's shoulder. "Adios, amigo. Watch yourself." Rafael gave him a thumbs up and grinned. Ginger nodded, and Connor led Maggie between the tables and out into the packed street.

In the confusion and noise there was no way to talk, so Maggie grabbed Connor's arm and held tight while he turned at Hidalgo Street and maneuvered their way a couple of blocks to the Hostal de la Noria, where inside, they left the crowd behind.

"They have one terrific *pollo a la plancha* here," Connor said. "If you're that hungry."

Maggie was starved and hadn't known it. "Peanuts and red wine won't do it," she said, and laughed. They sat in the atrium courtyard, the air now soft and cool. The place was lovely, the walls plastered smooth and painted shades of purple and yellow. Eggplant and mango, Maggie thought. Huge terra cotta pots tied with hemp ropes overflowed with ferns, hung from the rafters.

This is the sort of house I want, she thought, and smiled. A sad smile, she knew. Dream on, Maggie, dream on.

They ordered. Connor knew the waiter (did he know every waiter and bartender in town? Maggie wondered), and neither of the men even glanced at the menu. On certain days, in a certain mood, this would have grated on Maggie. Or maybe with a different man. Connor knows what he likes, Maggie reasoned, this pollo specialty. He's still part overgrown kid, excited to share his discovery with me.

Maggie sipped on a lemonade and spread butter on half a bolillo. She knew what mattered to her, where to draw the Maggie-line, how to take care of herself. She kept her camera between them, resting on the table. Her hotel was only a few easy blocks away.

And Connor? She would wait and see. He didn't seem in a dancing mood right now, and later might be embarrassed by his talk about waltzing. He seemed to be a strange and complicated, probably conflicted, man. Not a bad person though. Not perfect, never even nearing that. But perfection no longer interested her, even if commitment did.

Gordon had pretended to the throne of perfection, an act that ended in pretense and illusion. Maggie would settle for a few obvious and admitted flaws any day.

"What was going on between you and Ginger?" Maggie asked.

The waiter set their pollo a la plancha before them, and for a minute Connor studied his plate, then stirred the sauces that filled two small bowls. "Oh, a little difference of opinion about things. Her watercolor, oversized, dwarfed the student's art, and she already had eight or ten of her lithos in the gallery. Plus the way she acts around Rafael, I guess." Connor spooned some of the salsa verde over one end of the thinly pounded and grilled chicken. Then he spooned some chipotle sauce over the other end.

"Indecision," he said, nodding towards his plate, "because I always want the very best of everything. I'm afraid that if I say yes to one thing," and he dipped the spoon once more into the green sauce, "then I'll be saying no to everything else."

He looked over at Maggie. With his earnest look, Maggie thought. She had seen it before, but tonight it was different and seemed more authentic. Or maybe Maggie wanted it to be.

"But right now," he went on, gesturing with his fork, "I'm more than a little tired of my bullshit, my complaints." He speared a bite of chicken and pointed to the chipotle sauce. "My favorite." He chewed for a moment, then nodded his approval.

"Anyway, I'm damned sure glad I'm here, with you, and not back there with Ginger and Rafael. Sometimes with her I don't know what in the hell to say or do."

"You'd figure something out, I bet," Maggie said.

Connor felt himself flush.

"You blushed," Maggie said. "I can't believe it, but you did." Behind his gruff exterior Maggie thought she had glimpsed Connor as he might have been, maybe years ago, as an innocent boy. But it was hard to imagine Connor ever being innocent. Complex, yes, and awfully hard for her to read. She reached over and touched his arm. "It's okay to feel uneasy around the two of them. And I can see how you might have a whole mix of feelings around Ginger. I think Rafael's cute, too."

Connor raised his eyebrows and laughed. "You women," he said.

"Not much different from you men."

Oh, hell, Connor thought. This woman sees right through me, and doesn't hesitate to call me on it.

By the time they left Hostal del Noria the streets had thinned out. They walked back slowly, meandering through the zócalo, and found a bench that faced a sluggish fountain.

"First bench I've sat on here," Connor said. "They're always either jammed or splattered with bird crap." He laughed uneasily and felt himself straining to make small talk, to somehow keep the night going, not let it end.

Maggie sat quietly. She scanned the windows of a hotel across the way. Most of the rooms were dark, but here and there a room glowed from a late-night television. "Our campfires," she said.

"What's that?" Connor turned to her. But she didn't answer, and for a long time they stayed there under the washed-out flicker of a distant street lamp, silent.

Finally, Maggie took Connor's hand. "I'm a big person," she said. "You're a big person, too."

Connor laughed. "I guess I am," he said. "Although sometimes I don't act like it."

"We two are big, grown-up people." Maggie stood and helped pull Connor to his feet. She pointed down Independencia, past the sitio where a couple of taxis waited in the dim light. "Las Golondrinas. Just follow the steps up the hill. Room 22. My room." Maggie hesitated a moment. "Give me twenty, maybe thirty, minutes." She looked quizzically at Connor. "Are you okay with that?"

"Yeah," Connor said. "I'm better than okay. That chipotle sauce took care of the mezcal, I guess."

"I don't mean that," she said. "Are you okay with me?"

A gang of young boys raced across the far corner of the zócalo, yelling, and Connor turned to watch them disappear. "Maggie, I want you," Connor finally said. "I know you and I want you."

"Room 22," she said again. "Through the front office—don't let Geronimo intimidate you—just tell him you're my friend. Or, better, I'll tell him to watch for you, to let you in. Twenty-five minutes," she said again. "Okay?"

"Ten minutes," Connor said. He didn't grin.

Maggie ran her fingers around Connor's neck and pulled him close. She kissed him lightly on the roughness of his cheek and gave his hand a squeeze before she moved away. "Twenty minutes," she heard Connor whisper. Maggie smiled, but didn't turn around. Then his voice rang louder, as if he no longer cared who might hear. "I want you, Maggie O'Neill."

Maggie ran up the last few steps to the hotel door. Geronimo, behind the front desk, listened with one eye on the little tv while Maggie stumbled over her words. Then he nodded. "Claro," he said, and settled back in his chair.

"Yes," Maggie heard Michelle say, all the way from Houston. "Yes, yes, yes!" Maggie hurried up the stairs to her room. She stopped at the door to catch her breath. "Michelle," she said. "I don't think I'll be needing you anymore."

Now she wanted to slow things down, so that she would remember this night. In her room Maggie quickly showered, keeping her hair dry as best she could. She tossed clothes in the closet and slipped on a softened and fad-ed-to-gray T-shirt that doubled for pajamas. It fell halfway down her thighs. She checked the mirror.

But just then Connor knocked, lightly. Oh damn, she thought, and glanced in the mirror once more and shrugged. "The best I can do," she whispered, but nodded her approval.

"Just a minute," Maggie whispered through the door. She moved across the room and lit a candle. Too much, too contrived, she thought, and blew it out. She turned toward the door. "Okay Connor. Come on in."

Connor closed the door behind him. "Did I hurry you too much?" he said. "That damned bench got awfully hard. And I didn't want to wait."

Maggie smiled and Connor moved toward her. His eyes moved from her T-shirt to the bareness of her legs. He tossed his hat in the direction of a chair and moved close, touched her neck lightly with his fingers, then held her by both wrists and kissed her eyes, one and then the other.

"This is not fair," Maggie said, and pulled away. She unbuttoned his shirt and he slipped off his boots, his jeans, and then they fell onto the bed.

"You sure this is all right?" Maggie murmured, knowing that it had to be, that by God she wouldn't stop now. "I'll kill you if you say it's not."

Connor laughed and sat on the side of the bed. He pulled off his socks and then stood facing Maggie and stepped out of his shorts. He stood there a moment, eyeing the dresser where Maggie had lit and then blown out the candle. He moved quickly across the room in the half-dark to the dresser. From a vase that held a bouquet of watercolor brushes, he chose one, checking the bristles for softness.

Connor moved back to the bed and Maggie watched, saw his body, the body of a man in his forties who seemed to be at ease with his nakedness.

He eased onto the edge of the bed, bent down, and kissed Maggie once more. She reached for him, but he shook his head, took her arms and moved them to her side. She lay still and waited.

Connor began at her ankles, running the soft bristles of the brush over the contours of her legs, first one then the other, moving the brush lightly, as if he were painting Maggie with a light wash. With his thumbs he pulled at her shirt and she lifted her hips to let him slide it up almost to her breasts. Then he brushed her thighs, slowly, like the artist that he was, painting the outside first and then, when Maggie parted her legs, he brushed the inside of her thighs with long, even strokes. In a moment he moved the brush slowly to her mound of softness.

Maggie bit her bottom lip, tilted her head back a little. She reached for him again, and this time he didn't stop her.

He pulled at her shirt again, taking it farther up, and she raised up enough for him to pull it over her head. Maggie ran her fingers through her hair, then lay back and waited.

Connor tossed the brush aside and kissed her breasts. "God, you're beautiful, Maggie," he said. And now he moved quickly, not wanting to wait for anything. She pulled him to her, and when he kissed her the salt from her tears surprised him.

CHAPTER 20

The sky hinted at the day to come, not yet blue but a wash of muted gray, when Connor moved down the stone steps and pushed out through Las Golondrinas's outside doors and into the Oaxacan morning. The street sweepers, out every morning, now moved down Hidalgo with their brooms of bundled branches, pushing last night's trash before them with great arcing sweeps that rattled rhythmically across the cobblestones. A lone taxi driver leaned against the door of his cab and studied the day's sports news in the local paper. He didn't lift his head when the gringo hurried by.

It was a good six-block walk from Maggie's hotel to the gallery on Alcalá, and Connor hoped to get there before the Señora was about. Do you never get over that feeling, he wondered, that sex with a new woman is illicit? Something to hide?

Or was that his old habit of going to any lengths to avoid complications, avoid conflict—old intuitive reactions that could hardly help anymore. He felt as if he and Maggie had gotten away with something, pulled one over on . . . whom? Maybe the world in general, he thought, and a grin crossed his face.

Connor planned to brew his coffee, then show up at Rafael's as usual. He would visit for a few minutes with his young friend, and then go down and say good morning to Señora Velez. No class until Friday, when a new bunch of students would show up, he hoped. Then he would retreat to his room and sack out for a couple of hours and try to recover from his mostly sleepless night. He would meet Maggie at one for a *comida corrida*.

Connor eased through the courtyard, then made his way up the circular stairs toward his room. Across the way he could see that Rafael's door was already halfway opened, but the room was dark, and Connor slipped into his own room without being seen.

He felt a little queasy. The night would catch up with him, he knew, and his hand shook a little when he spooned the coffee into the basket of the drip pot. He showered while the coffee brewed and stayed under the hard spray, breathing in the steam until the water began to cool. After his first sip of coffee he felt restored, almost normal.

He dressed—clean jeans and a fresh laundered shirt—and checked himself in the mirror; a little worn-down, but not much more than usual. Connor filled his cup again and moved out to the balcony. Few things I do well, he thought, but I can make a damned good cup of coffee.

He glanced at Rafael's door, still half-open, and moved slowly around the balcony, the usual routine so that Rafael would hear him coming. He scuffed his boots lightly on the stone as he walked, stopping for a moment, clearing his throat of some morning congestion, and took another sip of coffee as he moved along.

Later, he would tell this to Maggie, and somehow it helped, the telling being a way of distancing him from what happened. A way for Connor to step back from that place and time and protect himself. Something only later that he understood.

As he moved those last steps to Rafael's door, Connor hoped that his young friend might have an extra pan dulce for him, something he could munch on with the last of his coffee.

But the way he remembered what happened next, the way later he told it to Maggie, seemed to be a horrible dream, something outside of time altogether.

"Rafael," he told her, and then had to stop a moment, for he had seen his young friend hanging there, in the middle of his room, from a rope stretched taut, knotted around the water pipe that ran across the ceiling, and then down, the rope ending in a loop tight around Rafael's neck. Rafael's bare feet dangled a few inches above the floor.

At that moment Connor fought to breathe, the wind knocked from his lungs by the sight. Quickly he recovered and with a grunt lifted Rafael, held his body up to take the weight off his neck, holding him suspended, Connor's face buried in Rafael's stomach.

Connor remembered that smell, but he couldn't tell Maggie this; he could never tell anyone else, and even then knew that the smell of Rafael's death would live with him from then on.

Connor held Rafael that way, taking on his full, dead weight, supporting him until his arms cramped, and he had to let Rafael's body drop once again.

Connor remembered that moment, for he heard what seemed to be a sigh, an exhalation from Rafael, but later realized that he couldn't have sighed, for he had been dead, it turned out, for hours. So the sigh must have been Connor's own.

He stumbled back into the light of the balcony and yelled something incoherent—later he remembered that incoherence to be the way a man might cry out in his sleep, jolted awake from the grip of a nightmare.

But there was no awakening for Connor, and he sank to his knees, his hands gripping the cold railings of the balcony, and with his voice filled with pain, he called for someone, anyone to help. Then he retched, spilling his sourness over the smooth indifference of the stone.

The city police came later and in no great hurry, for, as one of them explained with a shrug, Rafael was dead. Three of them in uniform, and the one who was the *jefe*, who introduced himself as Ulysses, questioned Connor.

Connor answered his questions honestly: No, he had heard nothing during the night, and no, he had not seen any strangers on the balcony around Rafael's room. Ulysses was the smallest of the three men and wore glasses with flip-down shades that he moved up and down as he asked the questions.

Connor did not volunteer about his night with Maggie at Las Golondrinas, or the early morning hour that he had returned to his room. As far as he was concerned those details were none of the jefe's business.

Ulysses finally shrugged and gestured that Connor could go. Back in his room he stripped away his fouled clothes. He would toss them, never wear them again. When he kicked his shirt into the corner of the room next to the door, he noticed streaks of blood across its front. He checked his arms and chest for a cut or a scrape, but nothing there.

Connor showered, scrubbed his arms and face and his chest until his skin burned and the water ran cold. Shivering, he dressed once more and ventured back over to Rafael's room. The three policemen were still there, in the middle of a conference. Two other men had shown up with a stretcher and a thin blanket. They waited, sitting at the top of the stairs, and smoked. Ulysses turned when Connor came in. Rafael's body, still on the floor, had been covered with plastic sheeting.

"You have a question?" he asked Connor. "Something else to tell us?"

Connor nodded. "The blood. What about the blood? It was on my shirt, you know. Where did that blood come from?"

Ulysses gestured with his head. "Come, I will show you."

Connor put his hand to his stomach and shook his head, no. He told the policeman that he was sick, and Ulysses shrugged. Then he held out his arms and pointed to his wrists as he explained that something had cut Rafael's wrists. "Perhaps he hurt himself while working yesterday. Did Rafael cut the frames for the pictures in the gallery?"

"No," Connor shook his head. "Of course not."

"Perhaps he tried to cut his own wrists," Ulysses speculated, "and when that failed he hung himself."

"Hung himself?" Connor said. "What d'you mean? Rafael didn't hang himself. The last thing he would have done is hang himself. Someone must have tied his wrists, tight enough to cut them, maybe with some wire. Then hung him from the pipe, and when he was dead, cut the wire off his wrists."

Ulysses looked at Connor, bemused. "In your America, perhaps. Or maybe in one of your movies. But, here, we can only call it a suicide." He shook his head. "This is not murder. This is not the way one man kills another. Not here. Not in Mexico."

Ulysses motioned to the men on the steps with the stretcher. They flicked their cigarettes butts away and in a few minutes carried Rafael's blanket-covered body down the stairs.

Ulysses handed Connor a card. "Call me if you remember anything else. It is too bad. Just a boy from the country, but with some problems?"

"Problems?" Connor asked. "What sort of problems?"

"More than one," Ulysses said. "The security at the university said he was a troublemaker, started many of those protests when he should have been in class or studying. They asked us to, how do you say, keep an eye on him. Where he went, who his friends were."

"I was his friend. You watched me, too?" And Ginger and Maggie, Connor wondered.

Ulysses shrugged. "Whatever he did, we knew. That was our job." He shook his head. "These things happen. Now especially with the money problems people have. It is not uncommon. *Qué lástima*. We will contact his family; we know they live in Coyotepec. Also, his wife's family, here in the city." He turned away.

"Hey," Connor said. "Just a minute. You can't just leave it like that. Somebody killed him. And he was my friend. You can't just call it a suicide because it's easy."

Ulysses flipped up the shades on his glasses. "You can think whatever you like, Señor, but remember this. We do things differently here, and in the end we always get to the heart of the incident. We do not always know the absolute truth, but we always find the heart." Then Ulysses flipped down his shades and moved to the stairs, leaving Connor alone on the balcony.

Qué lástima, my ass, Connor thought. It's more than a goddamn Mexican shame. And that's it? That's all they will do? Connor eased down the steps slowly, full of anger and dread.

On the way out he said a few words to Señora Velez; they would talk about the art show later. "Life must go on," she said with a shake of her head as Connor turned to leave. Connor glanced around. Skeletons of all kinds from the Day of the Dead still hung here and there on the gallery walls. "But not always," he said, and he left, his shoulder brushing the black wreath as he moved out the front door.

That is what Connor told Maggie after he retraced his steps back to Las Golondrinas where she still slept.

"Poor Rafael," she said. "I can't believe it."

"I'm beat, but I guess we need to find Ginger," Connor said, "and let her know. As much as I hate to."

"Later," Maggie said. "She won't be awake yet. A couple of hours won't matter." Connor stretched out on the still-rumpled bed and Maggie stayed close, next to where he lay, until he faded into a deep sleep.

She was there, sitting on the edge of the bed when he awoke, dressed in her familiar Khakis and white shirt and lacing up her boots. "Do you want me to tell Ginger?" she asked. "I will, you know, if you're not up to it. For any reason."

But Connor went. He held Maggie's hand the four blocks over to La Mansion, and still held Maggie's hand while he spoke the words he had to speak to Ginger. Connor held Maggie's hand, not as a lover and not as a friend, but as a way for him to reach out and connect in some small way with a world that now seemed broken. Maggie put her arm around Ginger while the younger woman cried, and Connor could finally stay quiet and only watch.

In the early afternoon Connor followed the route he had taken weeks ago, following the band, finding his way to the house of Claudia's parents. His primary reason was to find out when the services for Rafael would be held, and this seemed the most straightforward way, but he was curious to see what their reaction had been to Rafael's death, if they had a theory or some idea that would provide a new insight into the tragedy.

Already a wide black bow hung on a post next to the gate that was open to the street. He held his hat in one hand and waved it to ward off a yellow hound that sniffed at his heels.

Esteban, Claudia's father, and two other men Connor didn't know sat under one end of the long overhanging porch. In the side yard Claudia's mother poked at a pot of clothes that boiled in a black pot over an open fire.

Connor stopped in the yard, and Esteban moved out of the shadow of the porch and raised his hand in greeting. The other men moved into the darkness of the house. They talked. Yes, Esteban remembered Connor from the night of the celebration. "A lot of mezcal," he said with a faint smile. The vigil had already started at Rafael's family home in Coyotepec, he said, and would last until the day after tomorrow, when mass and the burial would be held. "At about 11:00 that morning," he said. He stared down. "A tragedy, of course."

"Claudia and Carlos? Are they well?" Connor asked.

Esteban nodded towards the house. "They are here, where they should be, with their family—with us—where they belong." He glanced around. "Rafael, you know, was a good boy in his own way, but he did not always take care as he should have. Not of himself, not of my daughter and my grandson." Esteban stopped for a moment, and Connor had the feeling that he was waiting for him to agree or not. Connor stayed quiet.

"Claudia's in-laws," Esteban continued. "Rafael's family—well, what can I say? They are different, not always as gracious as one would hope. Often in bad times such as this people say things and act in ways that are foolish. But I will try to understand."

"Is Leonardo here?" Connor asked. "He had treated me well the night of the fiesta."

Esteban shifted his feet and looked around. "At Miahuatlán, selling a load of cedar posts. Yes, Leonardo has been there all week. I will try to contact him, but that is not easy."

Connor shook hands with Esteban and left. But at the gate he stopped and gazed down the street where on that night Rafael had come to where Connor now stood. Rafael had waited for Claudia, and she reluctantly, or angrily, had walked out to see him. Then Leonardo rushing out to confront Rafael, and the shouting and crying echoed through Connor's mind.

Bad blood between these two families all along; that was easy to see. And now this. Qué lástima, Connor thought. What a pity, the wars between families can be brutal, and he began making his way back to the gallery. But could Leonardo have killed his sister's husband? Connor didn't think so, but he didn't know Leonardo all that well, and he didn't always understand the prices one paid in Mexico.

Maggie was waiting for him by the fishpond when he got back, and for a few minutes they sat on the wide stone rim and watched the koi move lazily around. Connor wondered who would feed the fish now that Rafael was gone. Maybe he should pick up some bread at the bakery down the street and scatter some crumbs in the pond.

Maggie had visited with Señora Velez earlier; the two of them walked through the gallery where the Señora already had some strange young man up on a ladder taking down the Day of the Dead decorations. "She really is being decent," Maggie said. "She was fond of Rafael, I'm sure, and she's sending flowers and food out to his family for the vigil. And the gallery will be closed until day after tomorrow, after the mass and burial."

"That's well and good," Connor said, "but Rafael's wife and kid aren't there," and Connor quickly caught Maggie up on his time with Esteban.

"What did the Señora say about the show?" he asked. "And the reception Saturday night? That life goes on?"

Maggie looked puzzled. "How did you know?"

Connor laughed, barely loud enough for Maggie to hear, the first time he had laughed that day. He had thought he might never laugh again. Maybe Señora Velez is right. Life does go on.

CHAPTER 21

Early, two mornings later, Maggie drove Connor out to Coyotepec in the Blazer. Maggie wore a black Mexican dress she had found at the Benito Juárez market the evening before, and a black reboso she had bought off a street vendor on her way back to Las Golondrinas. She had stopped in a shoe shop and found some black flats that were too narrow. She had hobbled around the shop. Oh my poor toes, she thought, but these will have to do.

It hadn't been so easy for Connor. In the mercado he finally found a white shirt with sleeves almost long enough for his arms and a pair of black slacks that a tailor there let out. At a stall next to the market he found a black felt hat, although he figured it would be in his hand most of the day.

"Johnny Cash," Maggie said now as they bounced along the rough road to Coyotepec. "Only more handsome, of course," she added.

"Of course," Connor agreed, and hoped.

Maggie and Connor had stopped at La Mansion the afternoon before and spent two more hours alone with Ginger on the patio. It was a going-away gathering, for Ginger was packed and would catch the seven o'clock Mexicana flight to Mexico City, and then the next morning on to Dallas, where her mother and sister lived.

Connor had picked up a Chilean bottle of red wine and some clear glass tumblers, and the three of them sat there and sipped the wine and talked, hidden by banana trees and enveloped by the scent of blossoming camelias and yerba santa.

While they talked Ginger sat facing the walkway that led in from the street, and Connor could tell she was uneasy, probably afraid. Finally she let it show.

"It wasn't suicide, was it," Ginger said, not a question at all.

"Was Rafael suicidal the last time you saw him?" Connor asked. He didn't need an answer and Ginger knew it, but she shook her head.

"Do you think," Ginger asked, "you know, that killing Rafael might not be enough? I mean, what about me?"

"No way," Connor said. "This is macho Mexican stuff. Revenge and family honor, that's what it's all about, the way I see it. You're inconsequential in this." Connor hoped he was right.

"Connor," Ginger reached out and touched his arm, the only gesture of tenderness or affection she'd ever extended to him. "You have to promise me this. That you won't let them get away with it, not by calling Rafael's death a suicide."

Connor didn't like to be held to promises, especially those he probably wouldn't be able to keep, but he put his hand on hers. "Sure," he said quietly.

"If I had only known," Ginger said—this, the third time she'd said it, and now Maggie interrupted. "But you didn't know. You couldn't have known. No way."

"But you can't kill somebody," Ginger said. "Not just because he's screwing somebody besides his wife." She looked at Connor, then over at Maggie. "That's all it was, dammit, screwing. Not worth this, for God's sake."

Maggie glanced at Connor then. She wondered about her night with Connor, if he would define their time in her room as "just screwing." Or would she?

"I didn't love him, you know," Ginger said. "I liked him. I liked him a lot. He was a lot of fun. A good man, too, but if I had loved him this all would have been different. I mean, it would almost be worth it." Then she sighed. "Oh, I don't know what I mean."

Connor thought he understood, that we would all act differently if we could know the price we would pay for our actions. Connor would have done things differently if he could have seen the future. He guessed he would have. But maybe not. Connor lifted his wine glass in a half-hearted toast. "To Rafael," he whispered, "my friend." Then it came time for Ginger to leave for the airport, and Connor and Maggie left without looking back.

In Coyotepec Maggie parked the Blazer at the church and moved slowly down the way to Joaquin's house, where cars were thick out front, some parked up on the yard and others stretching back on the narrow street, pulled off as far as possible. The yard was packed with people, and tables had been set up to hold the bowls and platters of food and bottles of all sorts of drinks. Out to one side a band tuned up, mostly off-key.

"So this is a Mexican vigil," he said quietly to Maggie as they reached the gate. "My kind of vigil, for sure."

Joaquin met them at the gate and gestured them in. He pointed to the house. "Rafael, his . . . you know. He is there, inside with the women."

Connor could hear voices from the house, but no wailing, no crying, just the rise and fall of a solemn sing-song chant, probably one of grief. Then one piercing sob blared out the open door, and Connor wondered if it been such a good idea to come.

Joaquin looked Maggie over carefully, and Connor panicked for a moment, afraid that Rafael's father would conclude that Maggie was the gringa who had caused so much anger and heartache.

"Your wife?" Joaquin asked Connor.

Connor hesitated a moment. "Yes, my wife, Maggie."

Maggie gave Connor a startled look.

He shrugged and whispered, "Easier this way," and she nodded.

Now others gathered round—Joaquin's other sons and two daughters and his two older sisters and one brother. Maggie nodded at each of them, then gave a little smile and wave collectively to all who had gathered there, all dressed in their best, all ill at ease, it seemed. Or maybe it was poorly suppressed anger.

Joaquin gave a satisfied nod, and gestured for Connor and Maggie to follow. But as he led them to a table of platters of tamales and bowls of stews, Rafael's mother burst from the house. She wiped at her eyes with an apron, and although her face was drawn and stained by tears, there was no tenderness about her; more an angry sadness. The worst kind, Connor thought.

She moved toward Maggie and Connor, made some guttural sound, and spun away to confront Joaquin. She barked something in Mixtec, all the while shaking her finger toward Connor and Maggie. Her voice clattered through the still air, and Connor took Maggie's hand as they backed away. He had a strong urge to cut and run while he still could.

Joaquin spit to one side and watched the wet blob dissolve into the sand. He said something sharp back to his wife, and everyone got quiet.

Connor hooked his arm into Maggie's arm. "Shit," Connor whispered to her. "This could be trouble city. Be ready to get the hell out of here." Maggie glanced down at her flats, her feet already aching.

Connor had visions of machetes flashing, and ears and more private parts being lopped off, scattered across the red sand of the yard.

But in a minute Rafael's mother gave a sigh and wagged her head. When she had disappeared back into the house, one of Rafael's brothers offered Connor a Modelo. Connor took a gulp and nodded his thanks. He offered Maggie the beer and she whispered, "Oh, yes." Murmurs of approval came from the men when she raised the bottle to all around and took more than a sip or two. The talk in the yard started up again as if nothing had happened.

The band began with some slow dirge-like music, a cue for Rafael's brothers to move single-file into the house. The band finished its song and waited. When no one came out of the house, they caught their collective breaths and passed around the half-liter jar of mezcal, then started up the dirge again.

Soon Joaquin's sons struggled out through the narrow doorway carrying Rafael's casket on their shoulders. They lowered the simple cedar box on an empty table under the overhang, then backed away, pulling at the sleeves of their shirts and brushing off their shiny pants.

Even from several feet away Connor could smell the fresh-cut cedar's sweet aroma. The women brought flowers, giant bouquets of long-stemmed lilies, fresh cut from a nearby creek bottom, all white, and laid them across the casket.

After that everyone stood around and seemed to be waiting for something. The men in the yard bunched up to one side near the water well, passing the jar of mezcal back and forth. The women stayed back on the porch or moved into the house with Rafael's mother. Their chanting started up once more.

Connor and Maggie moved to the fingered shade of the dead eucalyptus tree. "If the mezcal comes back around," Maggie whispered through a pleasant half-smile that she had for the morning fixed on her face, "Don't let it go until I get a shot, too. That chanting gives me the heebie-jeebies."

The band stopped, and the men carried their instruments to the shady side of the house where they squatted and smoked cigarettes and waited.

In a few minutes a pickup truck bounced down the road, dipping and rocking with the weight it carried. When the truck moved closer Connor could hear its squeaks and groans.

The truck was an old Ford, but it had been washed and polished; its green paint looked almost new.

Four men sat shoulder to shoulder in the cab, and a half-dozen more rode in the back. They rocked forward and then back in unison when the truck stopped out front. Esteban, Claudia's father, got out first, and he stood, looking around, his eyes moving until he spotted Joaquin. Then he nodded and stepped forward. The men in the back, a couple of them teenagers, scrambled out, moving stiffly in their dark slacks and white shirts and ties. They looked uneasy, wary, as they slapped the dust from their clothes, all the time glancing around at Rafael's kin in the yard.

One of the men who slid out of the cab was Leonardo, who somehow had magically reappeared from Miahuatlán. Connor recognized him at once, but Leonardo didn't acknowledge Connor. He had his eye on Rafael's brothers, who by now had all gathered behind Joaquin and were arguing quietly among themselves.

Maggie leaned close to Connor. "I know him," she said. "Or I mean I've seen him. That slender man in front."

"Who? Leonardo? From where? How?" Connor asked.

But before Maggie could answer, Esteban moved back to the truck and helped Claudia and Carlos out, followed by Claudia's mother.

Claudia wore a calf-length black dress, and a black net veil covered her face. Her low-heeled pumps gleamed dark against the red sand of the road. She carried one long-stemmed calla lily in her black-gloved hands.

Joaquin gestured for his sons and brothers to quiet down, and they all stood there for what seemed an eternity to Connor. Maggie glanced at him and rolled her eyes. Then pulled him back a little by one arm.

Without any apparent signal the band started up its sad song once more. Esteban gestured for his family to move to one side so the band could lead the way through the gate.

Joaquin said something in Mixtec and his boys lifted the casket and fell in behind the band.

The procession formed without another word, only a gesture from

Joaquin and then one from Esteban, as if they knew some correct, but unspoken, protocol.

Claudia went next, following behind the casket with the bewildered Carlos holding her hand. Claudia's mother hurried to join them.

Joaquin motioned for his daughters and wife to go next, and with a gesture cautioned her to stay back from Claudia. She scowled.

Then Esteban motioned for the others who had come with him in the pickup to be next in the procession, with the rest of his family behind. He nodded for Connor and Maggie to be next and they stayed back a little, not wanting to appear to take sides.

Joaquin and Esteban came last, the patriarchs walking deliberately, Joaquin trying to hide the limp from his bad leg, and Esteban going slowly, adjusting his pace to that of the other man while staring straight ahead, his eyes already fixed on the church.

The band wound down when they reached the closed front doors. Connor and Maggie held back, giving the two families some distance. Maggie slipped out of her shoes. "I hope you don't mind, but these are killing me."

Connor raised his eyebrows at Maggie. "Killing you?"

"Connor," she said with a suppressed smile. "This is a funeral. They're pinching my toes." She rubbed her bare feet on the smooth stones that led to the church. Once a kid, she thought with the shake of her head.

They stood there a few minutes, letting the band stash their instruments and the rest of the procession keep its division of families by moving farther apart.

Maggie turned to Connor. She quietly told him what she knew about Leonardo, how she had seen him, a small man dressed all in white who watched their table at Del Jardín the night Rafael died.

"Dammit, I was afraid of that," Connor said. "Don't say anything. I want to hear more, later."

Maggie nodded.

Connor wondered if they should tell Ulysses, or would that only complicate the tragedy? But Rafael didn't deserve to be killed. And now, even dead, he deserved justice.

The procession had bunched up at the entrance to the church. Joaquin and Esteban made their way to the front of the crowd and the doors swung open. Someone, the priest, he thought, in the front spoke rapidly, loudly in Spanish, but Connor was too far back to understand the meaning. He would have to rely on Maggie for that. Then a torrent of words in Mixtec that only could be coming from Rafael's mother. Connor grabbed Maggie's hand and she gripped her shoes in the other as they circled around the outside of the mourners where they could see.

A priest in his robes stood before the now-closed front doors of the church, holding a document of some kind high with one hand, waving it while he spoke. He was explaining something to Rafael's mother in Spanish, and to her sons, who still struggled under the weight of the casket.

Connor figured this was the priest he had heard inside the church when he and Rafael stopped by there on the fiesta day. The new part-time priest. He had a permanently indifferent, superior air, with an aloof, uncaring expression on his face. "That priest, he's a real prick," Connor whispered to Maggie. "Rafael told me all about him."

Rafael's brothers groaned and eased the casket down, resting it on the smooth slabs of stone. Joaquin limped up beside them. He spoke quietly, admonishing his wife to be silent. The priest listened, red-faced in the sun, moving his head from side to side at Joaquin's obviously reasoned argument.

He fanned himself with the legal-looking document.

Maggie listened as best she could, and after a couple of minutes she muttered, "Oh damn."

"What is it?" Connor leaned close to Maggie to hear, for now the whole group had started to shout.

"The priest won't perform the mass, since Rafael's death was a suicide. Church doctrine," he says. "The police in Oaxaca provided him with a copy of the death certificate. That's what he's waving."

"That certificate's not worth a damn," Connor said. "That's Ulysses. He has an agenda that I don't get."

Maggie shrugged. "It must be more complicated than that, but all those religious nuances are beyond me."

Connor nodded. "Damned Catholics," he whispered, and Maggie put her finger to her lips and squeezed his hand.

Joaquin said something to Esteban, and pointed across toward the wall that enclosed the cemetery. The two men turned back to the priest, but he shook his head, and wagged his finger at them while he talked. Joaquin slung his hat to the ground.

"Sacred ground," Maggie whispered. "The priest won't allow Rafael to be buried there."

The priest held up the death certificate once more and shook his head. "It is out of my hands," he said, and quickly retreated to the doors of the church and disappeared inside. The doors slammed shut once, then again more solidly.

Joaquin turned to face his wife and sons. "We do not need their church," he said. "And we do not need their little piece of land." He gestured toward the cemetery as if to dismiss it.

"I know the words that need to be said, and I own land where my son can be buried." He said something then in Mixtec. He drew a deep breath, and moving forward spat on the doors of the church. Claudia moaned and sank to her knees. She pulled Carlos close and sobbed.

One of Rafael's brothers shouted a curse at the doors of the church, then turned to Leonardo. "You and your brothers killed Rafael, and you will pay."

Leonardo lunged forward, but Esteban stopped him with his arm. "This is not a day for anger," he said. Then he spoke to his son quietly.

Joaquin limped right up to the doors of the church and with his good leg kicked against them. He shook his fist and uttered what Connor figured was the ultimate curse, for at that moment Joaquin's wife moaned, and she and her sisters and daughters started crying and wailing once again.

Joaquin ignored them all, and now he ignored Esteban, too. For Rafael was Joaquin's son and he must be given a decent burial. Joaquin gave a signal to the band and quickly they gathered their instruments and began to play.

Esteban helped Claudia to her feet, the brothers lifted the casket once again, and the procession moved slowly back the way they had come.

Connor and Maggie held back, found a bench to one side in the shade of a lone tree. There was no need for them to go on. Joaquin would take charge. Rafael would get a decent burial in the field beside his house.

"I'll have to tell Ulysses," Connor said, "about Leonardo, you know, watching us all at Del Jardín."

"I already did," Maggie said. "I didn't know Leonardo then, that the man in white was Claudia's brother. But when Ulysses surprised me by coming to Las Golondrinas, he asked me what I knew, if anything. I told him we had been watched. I thought he should know."

"Why didn't you tell me before?"

"I thought you had more than enough to handle," she said touching his arm, "without me piling on more. I didn't know what to do."

An old woman stopped by the closed doors of the church. She carried a single candle, and turned their way with a puzzled look on her face, as if the locked doors might be the two strangers' fault. She turned back and rapped on the doors, but no one answered.

"I asked Ulysses about Rafael," Maggie said. "I wanted to know the truth. If he thought Rafael was murdered."

"And?" Connor asked. "What did he say?"

"Well, he flipped down his shades so that I couldn't see his eyes. He told me it was a suicide. Straight-faced." Maggie sighed. "But I felt he knew it wasn't suicide, it was a murder. Not who did it. But I think he knows why."

Connor knew he should be angrier knowing that somehow justice had been sidetracked. It could have been Leonardo, with the help of a brother or two, for the family's pride, or it could have been the powers that ran the university and their security force, with Ulysses savvy enough to look the other way, while they made Rafael an example of what can happen to those who protest too much. For Rafael was older than most of the students, a charismatic leader, and not from an influential family. He would have been the perfect target.

But Connor felt drained, and right now it was too much to take in, still too many unknowns. Maybe this is justice of a different sort, he thought, just justice of a Mexican kind. Probably a different version of what the powerful can get away with all over the world.

Connor and Maggie sat silently then and watched as the procession began to file through Joaquin's gate. Then Maggie stood and took a few steps away and turned, facing the church. She couldn't watch anymore.

Connor couldn't bear to watch the slow procession, either, but it all began to play out in Connor's imagination: Rafael's family and Esteban with his clan again separated, while Joaquin would choose the place for Rafael's grave. Then his sons with picks and shovels would begin to dig. But when he imagined what would happen next, the casket being lowered, the pile of dirt shoveled back on the casket, Connor stood up. "I can't take this," he said. He turned back toward Joaquin's house, but could barely see the crowd.

"You don't have to watch," Maggie told him. "We're no help. They don't need us."

Connor continued to look toward Joaquin's house, just one of several lined up on the road. The little group of people gathered there seemed pathetic as they went about inventing a ritual to bury one of their own while trying not to kill each other.

"They need the priest," Connor said at last. "Damn it, as bad as he might be, they still need their church for this. What the hell is the church for if it won't help at times like this?"

Connor moved to Maggie's side. She still held her shoes in one hand, staring at the church, nodding to Connor that she understood. The longer he stood there, the more his anger rose. And then a strange thought came to him. If Connor could only get beyond those doors, then somehow he could make things better, the priest would change his mind, and Rafael's body could be interred in the cemetery. If Connor could get through those doors, that would break down whatever kept him from being more than a third-rate artist, a third-rate father, and a third-rate man.

"Stay here," he whispered to Maggie. "Something I need to do," and he moved closer to the church, eyeing the double wooden doors. The woman holding the candle watched Connor move her way and stop outside the church doors, and she backed to one side. He took a deep breath and knocked. He waited and knocked again, banged hard on one door with his fist. Then he called out in his bad Spanish and then in English, so if they were heard, the priest would have to understand Connor's words. "How can you close your door to your people, you son-of-a-bitch. What kind of a church, a priest, would do that?" Still the doors remained shut.

The old woman shook her candle at the doors, trying to help in her own way.

"You just hang on to your candle, sweetheart," he said. "I'll get you in."

Connor turned, took a dozen steps away, caught a glimpse of Maggie, and heard her say, "Connor." Then he turned. He stared at the doors for a few seconds. He tossed his hat to one side and started toward the doors again, his first steps a trot, and then with energy fueled by anger, he hit the doors with the most speed he had, shoulder first, and with a loud crack the slender metal strap-latch inside the doors gave way, and Connor crashed through. He rolled over once on the stone floor of the church and came to rest on his back.

Connor raised his head a little, looked around to see if the priest was there, but his shoulder hurt like hell and he eased back down again. He would wait right here until the priest came. He'll have to come sometime,

Connor thought, and besides, Connor didn't think he could move.

From down the way he heard the little band start up, but with a different sound that Connor had not heard before, a rhythm and a beat that must have echoed through these parts centuries before the Spanish even imagined this other world.

"Hell," he said, "Joaquin pulled it off, figured what to do without the damned priest."

Then he heard Maggie hurrying toward him, her bare feet slapping the stones as she ran. "You're a crazy man, Connor," she shouted. Oh Lord, she thought, do I need a crazy man in my life. Maybe not. But a good man who is sometimes crazy might have to be okay.

CHAPTER 22

Despite his sore shoulder and a scrape across his forehead, along with the depth of his hurt and a simmering residue of unresolved anger, Connor managed his way through his next class. But old habits persisted, even now, days after the funeral. Connor still took his first of the morning cup of coffee to the balcony outside his room where he could gaze across at the closed and locked door of Rafael's room, where a shred of wide, yellow plastic ribbon still dangled from the doorknob.

A little after 7:00 Alejandro appeared below, as if from nowhere, as if he had been doing this for years instead of days, walking his fat-tired girl's bike through the back gate and leaning it against the stone wall. He secured a brown bag to the handlebars (Connor thought, imagined, he could catch the aroma of fresh tortillas and soft-cooked beans) and gathered his tools from the downstairs storage room. He must have been aware of Connor watching from above, but never looked up. No acknowledgment of the gringo's presence.

Unlike Rafael, Alejandro seemed to be frail, old, and withered, at an age that could not be discerned. This man seemed to know that fixing his eyes on the work at hand, and that only, would keep trouble away. Something that Rafael must have known, but rebelled against.

But as Connor watched, Alejandro did talk, whispered for a few moments while he fed chopped fruit to the caged birds who croaked and cackled noisily back, in an attempt to mimic his words. And he spoke softly to the Koi as he tossed handfuls of dry dog food to where they swarmed.

Maybe Señora Velez was right, Connor thought. Life does go on. It has to go on. We require that, regardless, until it doesn't.

His watercolor class seemed a blur, Connor feeding on a reserve of repetition and feigned interest. But always he found his mind drifting to Rafael, from his first cup of coffee until he closed the door on the empty classroom at noon and hurried outside to Alcalá where he could wander away, anywhere but there. If Maggie were free and not obsessed with creating her book, they would meet for a late lunch, but not at Del Jardín. He marked that watering hole forever off his list of where to meet, to drink, or eat.

Somehow Connor got through that class the entire last session, and before it ended in early December, with Señora Velez's help, he found a small casita on a large property a fifteen minute bus ride north in San Felipe del Agua, the rent practically a gift from the Señora's wealthy owner friends from Mexico City. A quiet retreat for Connor, although often, after a late dinner with Maggie at Hostal de la Noria, he stayed in the city. With an intuitive understanding between them, just a touch of hands, or holding a glance, or an affectionate lean together of shoulders as they left the restaurant, he would walk her to Las Golondrinas some nights, and stay. They both taking and giving comfort.

They had a wordless agreement, a bond, to never speak Rafael's name. An agreement they honored, except once, when while moving up Alameda after dinner, two cars raced their way, and they stepped back to watch. It seemed to be two teenagers in a Mercedes followed by a newfangled Jeep overloaded with young guys. Music of some sort blaring, the boys yelling back and forth, one leaning out the window, pounding on the side of the car, hooting and more hollering, and then with a dual roar they were gone.

Without thinking, Connor muttered, "Cherry boys."

"What?" Maggie looked puzzled. "Cherry boys? What's that?"

Connor laughed for the first time in many days. "Oh, Rafael. That's what he called wild, rich, obnoxious teenagers." He shook his head and grinned. "I don't know where in the hell that comes from, and figure I wouldn't find out in one of Oaxaca's pricey language schools."

At that moment Maggie sensed some healing in Connor, the laugh, the grin, maybe just a beginning, but now she had hope. Although she also understood that his problems probably weren't rooted in Rafael's death, but were rooted more deeply. His young friend's death just caused things hidden away to simmer, still not quite bubbling to the surface. But time, she hoped, would take care of that, too.

More and more, Maggie found herself alone, deep in her art, the book of photographs and text beginning to come together, but now she felt diminishing returns from taking more photographs, so she stopped venturing out to the remote villages. Her early resolve to take the photographs straight-on, in focus, with no gimmicks she now saw might be a problem, too white-bread, so with help from the manager of the camera store in town she found a darkroom out at the university where she talked her way into access in off hours. If she supplied her own paper.

Her negatives were the clean slate she started with, then dodging and burning for shadowing effects and experimenting with focus to heighten, she hoped, their impact. While lost in the red glow of the darkroom she pulled from her memory something from Susan Sontag's *On Photography* that she had struggled through during her first museum class in Houston. Not verbatim, but one of Sontag's requirements for photographers was to "renew photographs with new shocks," in order to move beyond ordinary vision. Another: "The highest vocation of photography is to explain man to man." Both at that time seemed lofty and esoteric, over-intellectualizing what seemed to be a straightforward and simple process. But they stuck with her.

And now she perceived her work in a radically different way. Maggie would title her book "Lives of Loss" or maybe "Living with Loss." Something to convey that these maimed and damaged men were still alive, with the same needs and desires as ordinary, unscarred fellow villagers, but with lives complicated by their accidents. She finally got it. The text would be challenging, but now she was on her way.

Maggie and Connor made plans to be away from Oaxaca at Christmas, the mass of tourists during that holiday more than negating the loveliness of the quiet observances. Both of their visas would expire before too long, and they (after a tip posted in the tiny English language library) agreed that a trip across the Guatemalan border was much simpler, and more exotic, than driving north to the border of Laredo. The civil war in Guatemala had cooled down, and they could cross the border at the little-used Cuahtemoc crossing and spend one night at Huehuetenango, a doable three-hour drive, then pick up new 180-day Mexican visas and a new car permit on the way back out.

Already Maggie had imagined a follow-up project involving the women of those same villages who had to endure the too frequent drunkenness of husbands and the obesity and diabetes from sugared colas and Bimbo sweets that were spreading, affecting everyone, their children especially. Dr. Reyes had confirmed this near-epidemic to Maggie and encouraged her to document those emergent problems. The women in the villages already knew Maggie, the gringa woman who wore a man's trousers and always carried a camera, so access should be no problem.

She and Connor planned to meet in three days at Casa de las Bugambilias on Reforma for drinks and a light dinner and to finalize their plans. But Connor called a day early and left a message for her at Las Golondrinas. "Can we meet this evening, same place? Some news."

When Maggie made her way into the restaurant, Connor had found a corner table where they could talk in private. He had started on his shot of mezcal and a beer chaser. "Maybe, finally, some good news for me," he said when she sat down. A friend of his from grad school, someone he had corresponded with off and on for years, even from Oaxaca, had contacted him through Señora Velez at the gallery with a special delivery letter, and she had seen that it was delivered to Connor. This old friend was now the art department head at one of Houston Community College's far-flung campuses. "They need an interim art instructor," Connor told Maggie. She'd hardly ever seen him this excited. No more Mr. Cool. "Three classes, and due to my experience he can get me more than adjunct pay. And if it works out I would be first in line for a permanent faculty position next fall." He sat back and shook his head and finished off his beer. Maggie was afraid he was going to tear up. "This may be my last chance, and it's just in time. I had told the Señora I was done teaching there, after everything that happened." He shook his head. "And I think we were both relieved."

Maggie sat back in disbelief. "What—I mean, when will you have to be there?"

"Well, as soon as I can. I'll have to scrounge for a place to stay and get settled in, and see what courses I'm teaching." He took a deep breath again and reached for Maggie's hand and squeezed it. "I'm flying out, no bus, no way. Mexicana. And I wondered if I could make reservations for two. Or maybe we could drive out together."

Maggie, stunned, searched for words.

"You're done here, too," he said, "Just like me. You can finish your book in Houston, be easily in touch with publishers, and we can be together. Split the rent." He glanced at the table. "Oh, I forgot. Do you want a glass of wine?"

"Oh my God, Conner. That's great news. Margarita, no salt. That is a big break. I'm so happy for you. I don't know what to think." She gave herself a few seconds, while he got a waiter's attention, trying to put things in perspective.

Connor was relentless and on a roll. "And your son. Kelly. He'll be visiting his old man there in Houston, and I'll bet he'd like to spend some time with you. It's win-win. All the way around."

Maggie's margarita came, with salt, and with one finger she raked most of it into her napkin. "Can you listen a couple of minutes?" she said. "I have something I've been thinking, actually planning to do." And she went through her idea to document the women and children of the villages she knew, both how and why they live with drunken husbands, and children who gorge on sugared soft drinks and snacks. She stressed that it was something important to her, as an artist and as a woman. What she didn't say was that this gave her an odd combination of contentment and excitement that she'd never had.

"And my doctor friend," she said, "Dr. Reyes, here in Oaxaca, confirms the severity of it all—alcohol, obesity, and diabetes. And he backs me wholeheartedly."

Connor pursed his lips. He frowned, held two fingers in the air and glanced around for a waiter. "Not what I figured on," he said. "But, okay, we'll see what else we can work out."

But Maggie knew there was no other way. She wouldn't tell him that for almost all her adult life, and even before that as a child, a man had been telling her what she could and couldn't do. Her father early on, and then Gordon with his passivity and indifference and finally with his ten-year spreadsheet plan for her life had pushed her over the edge. Those men even had created situations to coerce her into going along, and she had conspired in her own discontent by remaining passive, silent. But no more. Maybe what she had thought on the day of Rafael's funeral, when Connor put his shoulder down and slammed through that church door and she ran toward him: "a good man who is sometimes crazy might have to be okay," was wrong. Not maybe. It was wrong.

"I really liked what we had," she said, hurrying to finish her drink. "It was working, was a good thing for me. At the time. And for that I have no regrets." Maggie shook her head. She reached over and took Connor's hand. "I guess it was unrealistic of me to think that this—both being here, what we had together—would go on, you know, happily ever after. Deep down, that's what I wanted. Oh, this is so hard."

She slid her chair back and stood. "But my life, my work—they are now tangled up with what is here, who I am. And I'm overjoyed with both."

Connor nodded, then stared off across the room.

"I so much don't want to hurt, to disappoint you. You've been through more than enough here already. But, I can't . . . " She shook her head.

Then from her purse Maggie pulled out some pesos without counting and dropped them on the table. "Come here," she said, motioning for him to stand beside her. "I could, we could," she said, "use a big hug." Connor rose and moved toward her. The last hug, they both knew. A hug they held for a long time.

Maggie moved through the restaurant, out the door and onto the sidewalk. She stopped and looked up and then down the street. Whichever way she decided to go, nothing stood in her way.

ABOUT THE AUTHOR

Photo by Lynn Watt

Donley Watt lives in Santa Fe, New Mexico, and is the author of five books of fiction. His collection of short stories, *Can You Get There from Here*, won the Texas Institute of Letters prize for best first book of fiction. He has traveled extensively in Mexico and lived for six months in Oaxaca.

CPSIA information can be obtained
at www.ICGtesting.com
Printed in the USA
FSHW021959210122
87843FS